THE SAFE HEART

Delphine's dream holiday in the South of France turns into a nightmare when she witnesses a murder. Placed in a 'safe house', she is faced with the dilemma of not knowing whom to trust. Handsome Commissaire Paul Dulac, in charge of her safety, would appear to be on the side of the villains. Her new boyfriend, Mark, is not exactly what he seems either. And what is the important evidence they seem to think she possesses?

JUNE GADSBY

THE SAFE HEART

Complete and Unabridged

LINFORD
Leicester

First published in Great Britain in 2004

First Linford Edition
published 2005

British Library CIP Data

Gadsby, June
    The safe heart.—Large print ed.—
Linford romance library
    1. Witnesses—Protection—France—Fiction
    2. Murder—investigation—France—Fiction
    3. Love stories 4. Large type books
    I. Title
    823.9'2 [F]

ISBN 1–84395–930–5

Published by
F. A. Thorpe (Publishing)
Anstey, Leicestershire

Set by Words & Graphics Ltd.
Anstey, Leicestershire
Printed and bound in Great Britain by
T. J. International Ltd., Padstow, Cornwall

This book is printed on acid-free paper

1

It was the way the sand scuffed up like that, all on its own in front of her nose, that gave Delphine goose bumps. It made a kind of 'phut' sound and a hole appeared as though a crab had just dived for cover.

She stared at the hole and gave a small, perplexed smile. When it happened a second time, realisation struck. That was no crab. It was a bullet. Two bullets, in fact, and somebody was shooting at her!

As a third bullet zinged past her ear, making a 'whee-ah!' sound, she realised that her leisurely breakfast on the beach terrace of her hotel was over.

'Delphine!'

She knew there must be a shameful dribble of milk on her chin, but she was too shocked to do anything about it.

Looking up, she met the startlingly

dark eyes of Paul Dulac. They were smouldering almost as much as the pistol he was holding inches from her face. A wisp of blue smoke trailed from the barrel and she smelled cordite.

'Get up!' he ordered sharply, his voice low and roughed with anger.

'Who the . . . ?'

Delphine started to ask him who he thought he was, ordering her about like that, but the hostile flash of his eyes told her to think better of it. She knew well enough who he was and even though she didn't like it, she was obliged to follow his instructions implicitly.

By the side of her chair she glimpsed a brown shoe, old-fashioned, well-polished. There was a foot in the shoe wearing a dark green sock. Above the sock, the end of a dark grey trouser-leg was visible. The owner of all this was lying on the floor. He wasn't moving.

'Don't look!' Paul ordered, hooking a hand under her armpit and hauling her unceremoniously to her feet. 'Let's get out of here.'

'But isn't that Mr Armitage?' she protested feebly as he dragged her out of Sainte Maxime's Petit Hotel de la Plage and towards the big black official car that was parked conveniently at the entrance.

It was the Côte d'Azure at the height of the summer season. The sun poured molten heat down on to the heads of the tourists, and the sea was an inviting shade of turquoise. And Delphine was supposed to be on the holiday of a lifetime, tasting the nightlife and the 'beautiful people' haunts and looking for an adventure to make her forget a disastrous relationship. What a disaster that had turned out to be.

⋆　⋆　⋆

Everyone had told her it was wrong to come on her own. There'd been such stories in the newspapers lately, stories to make the hair on the back of the neck rise — girls being abducted.

'But they're just the stories we hear

about,' she had argued. 'There are millions of young women walking about in the South of France who are perfectly safe.'

Nothing would put her off. It would have taken an outbreak of World War III to make her change her mind. After her experience with Tom Denning, nothing was going to get her heartbeat above a feeble flutter.

However, she had always dreamed of coming to this part of the world one day and, yes, in that dream there was always the ubiquitous rich and handsome hero.

It was such an unfortunate coincidence that she should decide to take a walk in the moonlight two nights ago. It was a chance in a million that she would turn a corner at five in the morning because she couldn't sleep — and witness a murder.

Not only that, the killer had turned and looked right at her and his features were forever imprinted on her mind.

For a brief, scary moment, Delphine

thought the man was going to turn on her and kill her like the poor individual at his feet. However, a patrolling police car had cruised by just as Delphine opened her mouth and let out a scream that ripped through the silence of the dawn.

They had chased after him, but he quickly merged in with the shadows. Delphine was immediately whisked off to the office of a stuffy police headquarters building, bustling with agents de police and gendarmes. People were bombarding her with questions in rapid French, which she didn't understand. Her hesitant, schoolgirl French had deserted her.

They eventually took her back to her hotel and told her not to leave, that they would be in further contact. The man in charge had muttered something about protection.

A few hours later, Paul Dulac turned up with his dark, unfathomable eyes and his sensuous but unyielding mouth. And he disturbed her most of all. He spoke near perfect English, but with just enough accent to make his deep voice more interesting.

She was, he informed her, not only the sole witness of an odious crime, but she could identify the man responsible, which put her own life at risk.

'I am your keeper,' he had said with a sardonic smile.

2

That had been yesterday and he had virtually kept her prisoner in her room ever since. He was probably furious with her for slipping down to the terrace when he left her unattended for a few minutes while he attended to some official business.

'Will you please get into the car!' Commissaire Paul Dulac was yelling at her now, and forcing her into the back seat of the car, his big hands clutching at her, gripping so tightly that she thought he was about to rip off her flimsy sundress.

'Stop that!' She fought him off, slapping at him mercilessly and kicking out with her bare feet, though his shins were rock hard and she thought it probably hurt her toes more than it hurt him. 'What are you trying to do, for goodness sake? Kidnap me?'

'Not exactly, Mademoiselle Harvey.'

Suddenly he was addressing her formally again, as he had when they first met two days ago. It made him seem more officious and less of a handsome, continental gigolo. 'Actually, I'm trying to save your life, but you do not seem to be worried that people are trying to kill you.'

Delphine stopped struggling and gave a loud gulp, her saliva sticking in her throat.

'Was that bullet meant for me? I mean, the one that killed that nice old man?'

'Mademoiselle . . . Delphine!'

He looked at her despairingly.

'I fired the bullet that killed your 'nice old man'.'

She stared at him with horror-filled eyes, licked her dry lips and glanced back at the hotel, wondering if she could make a dash for it and lock herself in the room until they sorted out this horrible mess she found herself in.

'You killed Mr Armitage? But . . . why?'

'Because I recognised him from CIA

file images sent to us via the Internet. He was the right-hand man of Tony Borgheza — a mafiosi godfather who just happened to be spending his vacation in the hotel next door. That was the man whom you saw . . . '

Delphine drew in a gasp of hot, mid-morning air tinged with the heady perfumes of rose blossom, bougainvillea and warming rosemary.

'The man who was murdered?'

'No. The man who did the killing. Very unusual, doing his own dirty work.'

Delphine forced a small, uncertain laugh and tried to sound derisive.

'Oh, come on! I mean, this is tourist country. It's civilised . . . '

'We are only as civilised as the people we allow to live in our country. Now, Delphine, would you please do as I say and get into the car?'

'I don't have any of my things. Where are you taking me?'

'To a refuge — I think you would call it, in England, a safe house.'

'Oh, that's brilliant, just brilliant!'

Delphine felt so shaken and angry that she actually banged the car roof with her fist and stamped her foot, gagging with pain as she trod on a sharp stone. 'The least you can do is let me pack my bags . . . '

'The car, Delphine! Now!'

Delphine got quickly into the car.

It had not struck her until then that she was no longer a tourist, but a fugitive. Not a fugitive from justice, but from crime of the worst sort.

And the perpetrator of that crime, whoever he was, was certainly not putting on an act.

He had definitely meant business when he beat that poor man's head to a pulp.

★ ★ ★

The victim was a local businessman, they had told her, not wishing to divulge any further details at this stage. He had been foolish enough to get involved with the mafia in the States.

Realising, too late, what he was

getting into, he had tried to pull out. But already he knew too much, just like Delphine did now.

'Why did you kill him?' she asked as the commissaire climbed in beside her and gave a sharp order to the driver of the car to go vite, vite, vite!

'Your Mr Armitage?' Paul Dulac gave her a sidelong glance, but all the while his eyes were scouring the pavements, delving into shop doorways, glancing up at hidden windows. 'Because when the two bullets that were meant for you missed their target, he was about to put a knife in your back, a rather long, slim-bladed flick knife that I saw him take out of an ankle holster.'

'Oh!' Delphine gasped and licked her dry lips. 'I didn't see. He was behind me.'

'Exactly. You would have felt a sharp prick, no doubt, then nothing, not even the sun you like to soak up, or the sea you like to float in. You would no longer see the flower you admire so well or hear the birds you feed with crumbs on your balcony.'

'I hope they pay you well to be a spy. It must be horribly boring playing nurse-maid.'

Now the smile did reach his eyes and he laughed out loud. It was such an attractive laugh that Delphine almost forgot that she was supposed to hate him.

'Not a spy, Delphine, just a police-man — and you are anything but boring,' he said, running long fingers through his thick, dark hair and showing a small expanse of muscular forearm. 'As a matter of fact, I find you quite fascinating. I keep wondering what I shall have to do next to keep you safe. You certainly do not seem to be aware of the seriousness of your plight. Or do you?'

Delphine shrugged and leaned away from him, looking out of the brown, polarised window at her side.

★   ★   ★

The Côte d'Azure scenery flashed by in a haze as the car picked up speed. Four days was all she had enjoyed, then this had to happen, just as she had met someone who showed promise, too.

It wasn't long before they left the long, busy coastal route and headed inland on quieter roads to the foothills of the Alpes Maritimes.

It seemed a long, circuitous journey, most of it driven at speed with corners taken almost on two wheels and rubber often squealing and melting into the road surface.

'I suppose he knows what he's doing.'

Delphine gasped out her words as she fell about drunkenly in the back seat, grabbing anything she could to steady her.

'Gaston trained long and hard to get as good as this,' Paul said in a strangely low voice that told her his back teeth were every bit as gritted as hers. 'If anyone can lose a tail he can.'

Delphine blinked up at him and felt a ripple of something more than just fear course through her as their eyes met.

'We're being tailed? This is just unbelievable.'

'Don't worry. Gaston will lose him.'

The big Frenchman laughed softly then winced and looked down at her left hand, which was clamped on to his broad, muscular thigh.

'You are not, I hope, seeking to open the main artery in my leg? I know you do not like me — you've made that perfectly clear, but I beg of you, my poor English chaton, have pity on my body.'

With a tiny embarrassed cry, Delphine withdrew her hand and turned even more away from him, clinging with both hands now to the safety belt that was almost choking her it was so high and tight across her chest.

As if she would want anything at all to do with him or his body, she told herself with a spasmodic jerk of one shoulder.

Men were such conceited creatures.

★   ★   ★

Five minutes later she stole a glance in his direction and decided that, after all, this particular man might have something to be conceited about.

It was almost indecent that any male creature should have such long lashes, such a straight nose and the most kissable mouth she had ever seen.

It was just like her to fancy someone so desirable and yet thoroughly unobtainable. It was the story of her life.

She had been in love with the idea of Tom, her ex-boyfriend, rather than Tom himself. That was obvious now, though at the time of their unprecedented separation two years ago she had been devastated. Her handsome, talented, explorer boyfriend had thrown her over for another.

Not wishing to bring back depressing memories, Delphine tried to lose her thoughts in the expensive upholstery of the car in which she was travelling.

She tried not to look at Paul Dulac, because she felt sure he was watching her and laughing to himself. She must really be the most pathetic person in police protection he had ever body-guarded.

'Nearly there!' Paul said over the velvety purr of the Peugeot engine.

She jumped at the sound of his voice, and even more at the feel of his hand resting heavily on her bare shoulder.

'Don't do that!' she grumbled loudly, pulling her shoulder away from the heat of his fingers and wondering what they expected her to do about clothes at this safe house they were going to.

She was practically naked with not even a lipstick to her name.

'Ah!' Paul seemed to breathe out a sigh of relief next to her and her shoulder felt cold where his hand had been.

'Is this it?' Delphine squinted forward in disbelief at the scattering of ramshackle, rustic buildings that had come into view at the end of the bumpy, rutted track, which threatened to dislodge more than just the car's innards. 'I don't believe it!'

'Believe it,' Paul said with a wry

grimace. 'This, Delphine, is going to be your home for — well, as long as it takes.'

Maybe she swore out loud without realising it, because he was chuckling to himself as he opened the door and helped her out. And her hand lingered far too long in his, possibly because he wouldn't let go — or perhaps because she didn't want him to.

Either way, there was an uncomfortable tingling in the centre of her palm that radiated all the way up her arm to her heart and ended like the thump-thump-thump of a bongo drum in some dark and distant jungle.

3

The house was rustic, to say the least. Its wattle and daub walls were crumbling between ancient crossbeams blackened by age, open wood fires and generations of cooking with duck fat. In fact, there was an odour pervading the musty air that spoke of French country living going back centuries.

Paul caught her eye and gave her a secret smile. Delphine felt sure he was reading her mind and was highly amused by the thoughts that were running through it.

'This is Gaston's family home,' he said and Gaston turned from sweeping a squawking chicken off the long, scrubbed oak wood table in the centre of the room and grinned at her proudly.

'Chez moi!' he told her, jabbing a thumb into his chest.

Delphine turned at the sound of feet

scuffling on the dusty floorboards and saw an elderly woman who could have been anywhere between sixty and eighty. She was grey-haired, slightly bowed and her parchment skin bore the lines that told of hard working in the open air.

At first, the woman seemed to be scowling, but then, as her eyes alighted on Delphine, she beamed a warm smile of welcome. Clasping Delphine's hand and nodding vigorously, she led her to a stout, wooden chair and invited her to sit down.

'You are honoured, Delphine,' Paul told her in a low voice as the woman scurried off. 'Madame Lacoste had placed you in her husband's chair — the one he carved himself. Not even Gaston is allowed to sit there.'

Delphine's face dimpled into a weary grin.

'Well, as long as Monsieur Lacoste doesn't object — it's very comfortable.'

'My papa — he die.' Gaston provided the information with a grave expression, then immediately winked at her.

Delphine took the heavy tumbler that the woman handed her and watched as the old, work-worn hands carefully poured out a measure of cloudy red wine from a stoneware carafe that must have served generations of her family.

Far from being a connoisseur, Delphine sniffed suspiciously at the liquid that floated menacingly in her glass, aware of Paul Dulac's eyes on her all the while. The wine smelled fruity, so that was good, she thought.

Everybody had been served and glasses were raised to the call of, 'Chin!' and 'À la vôtre!'

The wine hit the back of Delphine's unsuspecting throat and made her cough. Through the noise she was making she could hear a cackle of laughter from her hostess and from Gaston. Paul was banging her on the back with an apologetic, but highly-amused smile lighting up his eyes.

'I'm sorry. I should have warned you. The Lacostes are famous for their strong wine.'

'Strong!' Delphine exclaimed when she could catch her breath and stop coughing. 'It would make a very good paint stripper.'

There was a quick exchange of French between Paul and Madame Lacoste and Delphine groaned silently to herself as she watched Madame refill her glass, nodding happily all the while.

'Is she trying to get me drunk?' she asked Paul and he chuckled and shook his head.

'No, but I am,' he said. 'You need to relax after what you've been through today.'

'Relax, yes, Commissaire, but I'd rather not get comatose, if you don't mind.'

A dog barked somewhere. Suddenly, both Paul and Gaston were on the alert, eyes flashing, heads turning, like two watchdogs expecting imminent trouble.

Which is exactly what they are, Delphine thought, taking another more careful sip of the wine and deciding that it wasn't quite as bad as she had first thought.

Another quick exchange in French followed, this time between the two policemen, and the old lady looked worried.

'What is it?' Delphine demanded, hating that she couldn't follow what was being said because they spoke so rapidly and it bore no resemblance to the Parisian French she had learned from the set of cassettes she listened to ad nauseum.

Paul Dulac held up a hand, palm towards her.

'Ssh.' Then to Gaston another flow of words and they left the room together, almost at a run, but being careful to be as quiet as possible.

Madame Lacoste made a sound like the escape of steam from a casserole and shuffled out of the room by a different door, muttering something about, 'Boys and their silly police games.'

There were the sounds of a scuffle

coming from outside in the yard. A human cry was muffled by the alarmed cluck of hens and the excited canine barking that had raised the alarm.

Delphine got up and staggered slightly as the rough country wine attacked her head and she remembered she hadn't had anything to eat today yet, her breakfast being so rudely disturbed.

She wondered if Mark, the young man she had met at the hotel, had missed her at lunch. He hadn't been there yesterday, so wouldn't know what had become of her. There hadn't been time, even, to leave a message.

Through the open window she saw clouds of dust rising as two bodies rolled, clasped in one another's arms, thrashing and grunting.

Then they came to rest and Paul Dulac stepped out and straddled them, his gun pointing at the head of one of the fighters.

'That is enough, monsieur,' he said harshly in English as Gaston pulled himself away and got unsteadily to his feet. 'Into the house, if you please.'

He reeled off a mouthful of French to Gaston, who nodded, brushed himself down and took out his own pistol before going off at a run, presumably to check that the intruder was alone.

Stumbling feet approached the living-room where Delphine waited, her heart beating slightly because of the unexpected excitement the brawl had caused.

Someone coughed and dust writhed through prisms of sunlight that streamed in through the open door.

'Mark!' Delphine gasped as a dust-covered figure almost fell into the room as if he had been pushed, which he probably had, by the commissaire's big hand.

'You know this man?' Paul Dulac's forehead creased and he regarded her with narrowed suspicious eyes.

'Yes, of course I know him,' Delphine said breathlessly, taking her handkerchief out and applying it to the bleeding cut on Mark Easton's upper lip. He winced and tried to smile, but gave it up as a bad job.

'Hello, Delphine,' he muttered, fingering his jaw tenderly where a bruise was already spreading. 'Are you all right?'

'That's not a question I know how to answer.' Delphine sighed deeply and turned her gaze on Paul Dulac. 'Did you have to be so brutal?'

'I'll speak to Gaston about it later.'

'There's no need to be sarcastic. It's very unbecoming in a man.'

'I'm sorry. I forgot that women have the prerogative in that department.'

Delphine flinched beneath the sharp black diamond stare and turned her attention back to Mark.

'What on earth are you doing here?'

'I saw them abduct you,' he said, speaking with difficulty as though his mouth were full of cotton wool. 'I should have called the police.'

Delphine pulled a face and inclined her head towards Paul Dulac.

'He is the police.'

'You're joking!'

Paul Dulac kicked the door shut behind him and stepped forward so that he was facing the fair-haired young man whom Delphine had known only a few days, but liked enormously.

'It is no joke, monsieur. And neither is the situation you find yourself now a part of. Please sit down. We need to talk.'

'What? Oh — um — yes — I'm sorry!' Mark stuck out his hand, then withdrew it again when it was ignored. 'I — I'm Mark Easton. Turnbridge Wells, England. Twenty-eight. Cambridge graduate. I work in — um — software — computers and the like. May I ask what this is all about?'

'No, you may not, for the present.'

Paul Dulac pushed Mark gently into a chair and Mark sat obediently, his eyes swinging curiously between Delphine and the policeman.

Gaston's mother appeared, wiping her hands on her apron. When she saw Mark's face she threw her arms up in the air.

Paul told the woman to bring some of her herbs to bathe Mark's face and she hurried to do his bidding.

★　★　★

Once the wounds on Mark's face and a large bruise over his ribs had been doctored in a mixture that smelled suspiciously like horse liniment, Madame Lacoste disappeared back into the kitchen and pans could be heard rattling as she went about her chores.

'Now, monsieur, I take it that Mark Easton is your real name.'

Paul was scrutinising Mark's face.

'Yes, of course it is!' Mark was affronted and showed it. 'You surely don't believe that I go around using false names, do you? What kind of idiot do you take me for?'

He winced at every other word and Delphine, feeling sorry for him, went to stand by him and placed a sympathetic hand on his shoulder.

27

She was instantly brushed away by the commissaire.

'For the moment, Delphine, I would prefer you to keep your distance from this man until I can verify his identify. Please sit at the other side of the room, not too close to the window. Over there, where I can see you and you do not make the perfect target for an expert marksman.'

Delphine gave a shudder at his words and sat down heavily on the chair he indicated, glancing fearfully towards the open window. She hadn't really felt afraid until his last words.

It had all been too ridiculously Hollywood and much too far-fetched to be believed. She rubbed at the goose-flesh on her forearms and stared broodingly at him.

Gaston came in on heavy feet that resounded on the stone floor.

'So,' Paul said, 'you came alone, Monsieur Easton.'

'There wasn't time to invite anybody else.'

'What are you doing here in France, monsieur? And how well do you know Mademoiselle Harvey?'

Mark blinked and looked perplexed.

'Mademoiselle Harvey? Oh, you mean Delphine! Well, actually, to answer your first question, I'm here on holiday, doing the tourist bit. As for the second question, I don't know Delphine very well at all, but I had planned to put that right this evening because — hang it all, do I have to spell it out for you. She's quite a dish, in case you haven't noticed.'

Paul Dulac turned and raised an eyebrow at Delphine and she felt herself shrink inside her sundress as his eyes travelled over her with deliberate slowness as he drank in every inch and every curve, missing nothing.

'Hmm. Yes, I had noticed. It would be difficult not to, non?'

'Oh, please!' Delphine managed a derogative groan and turned her face away so he wouldn't see that she actually felt quite flattered by his remark. But then, she had done exactly the same in the hotel bar the first night when she had been chatted up by Mark, not wishing to seem too eager.

Paul, who had been scribbling on a small notepad, tore off the top sheet and passed it to Gaston with an infinitesimal nod of his head. The police sergeant read it and pulled out his mobile phone. He was already speaking rapidly into it as he left the room.

He returned a few minutes later, during which time they had waited in silence, punctuated only by the sound of the crickets chirping outside and the hollow tick of the large grandfather clock built into the wooden panelling of the hall.

Paul took the sheet of paper back and, skimming it, gave half a knowing smile. He screwed the paper up and threw it in the fire that was crackling in the grate, despite the heat of the day outside.

'Interesting, monsieur,' he said. 'Very interesting. I'm told there is no such person as Mark Easton. At least, not corresponding with the age and the details you have already given me. Now, which one of us is lying, do you think?'

4

The soup that Madame Lacoste dished up for them at supper tasted a lot better than it smelled. For this, Delphine was infinitely grateful. She wasn't even put off by the fact that Gaston ate his like a builder mixing fast-drying cement. He dug, stirred, scooped, shovelled it in and swallowed at a nauseating rate. Finished well ahead of the others, he sat back, smiling his appreciation.

'You must excuse Gaston,' Paul Dulac said, wiping a piece of bread around his plate. 'He lacks finesse, but he is an excellent policeman.'

'Oh, God, I hate it when they do that!' Mark said from behind his napkin and squinted at Delphine through his already half-closed and discoloured eye. 'My mother would faint if anyone cleaned their plate like that at her table.'

'Your mother, monsieur, is not French.' Paul pushed his plate back and reached for the remnants of the wine in the large stone carafe, offering it first to Delphine, who refused. 'We French are a practical race when it comes to food and drink. It has been bred in us since the great Revolution. Perhaps even before. We waste nothing. In matters of the heart we take our time, but we are just as thorough.'

At this point Gaston's mother gabbled out a few words and pointed at the two young English people seated at her table, a look of good-humoured curiosity on her lined face.

'What is she saying?' Delphine asked, and Paul gave a low, melodic chuckle as he answered Madame Lacoste and she got up from the table, laughing like a hyena, to fetch a dessert of some kind that smelled highly of vanilla.

Paul leaned over to Delphine, his eyes twinkling.

'She wanted to know if you and young Mark here were lovers. I told her that the English were not known for their hot blood. They have ice and snow in their veins, fog in their brains and wind in their words.'

Mark pushed back his chair and looked around him.

'Quite the poet, aren't we? Where's the loo?'

'Gaston!' Paul raised his voice because Gaston's head was beginning to droop towards his chest. 'Show monsieur the facilities.'

'I don't need an escort to go to the toilet,' Mark objected, his cheeks flaming with embarrassment and anger.

'It has nothing to do with protection,' Paul said. 'We just want to make sure you don't escape.'

'You can't keep me here against my will, you know. You've got nothing at all on me, except your inefficient office can't find my file or something, so you've just decided that I don't exist.'

'Oh, you did exist all right. But if you are not Mark Easton, as you say you are, I'd like to know exactly whom

— and what — I'm dealing with.'

Mark sighed deeply and ran shaky fingers through his lank sandy hair that flopped immediately back over his forehead.

'I could prove I am who I say I am, but I haven't got my passport with me. In fact, I lost it the minute I arrived in France. Some pickpocket at the airport helped himself to that and my wallet. The hotel had to loan me some money to get by.'

He turned to Delphine and gave an apologetic shrug.

'That's why I wasn't too forthcoming when we met in the bar. I'm not normally a mean person, but . . . '

'That's quite all right, Mark. I understand.'

Paul gave an unyielding smile.

'You had better go to the bathroom. Madame Lacoste already thinks you are a spoiled little boy. I am inclined to agree with her.'

★ ★ ★

'Why are you so hard on him?' Delphine asked when Mark had left the room, accompanied by watch-dog, Gaston. 'I'm sure he's exactly who he says he is and quite harmless.'

'Are you, indeed?' He leaned across and tapped her arm with a long finger. 'Delphine, when you have been doing police work as long as I have, you develop a nose for things that are not right. I do not like this young man you have attached yourself to.'

'You sound exactly like my father,' she said and saw the quiver of an unbidden smile. 'Anyway, I'm not attached to him. We've only just met, but he's been positively charming and you've ruined what could have been a lovely evening.'

'And here was I thinking you were different from the other English girls we get here on the Côte d'Azure.'

He gave her another appraising look that made her quiver.

'Perhaps I am getting old. I do not usually make mistakes about people.'

'Nobody asked you to form an opinion on me.'

Paul got up and went over to close the shutters, ridding the room of the mellow evening light and blanketing the sound of the crickets and the frogs serenading one another.

'That is true, Delphine, but I formed it anyway. It is la mode — how do you say — fashionable — to pick up strange men in foreign countries.'

Delphine shot to her feet, almost toppling over her chair and making their hostess gasp and drop a piece of her pie on the table.

'I had no intention of that.'

'Oh, really? Delphine, the boy is not right for you.'

'You still sound like my father — or a jealous lover.'

There was a slight hesitation. He looked down at the table and played with a spoon, making whorls on the chequered tablecloth.

'I am sorry,' he said. 'But I am not available.'

'Oh! Well, that's all right, then, isn't it?' Delphine remonstrated silently with herself because there had been just a small flash of disappointment. She might have known that he was married. All the good ones were.

The good ones! That was a laugh. What made her think of him as a good one — a good man? He was too handsome, too brusque, too rude and too French.

5

'Tell me, Delphine . . . ' Paul seemed to have recovered from whatever was afflicting him and was again fixing her with a penetrating gaze that she found hard to get away from. 'How did you meet Mark Easton?'

Delphine accepted a piece of pie from Madame Lacoste, who patted her encouragingly on the shoulder then left the room.

'It was the day before I saw the murder in the alley,' she told him. 'I had just arrived. He was already there and since I didn't know anybody and knew nothing about the place, he was kind enough to show me the local sites of interest.'

'Did he tell you anything about himself?'

'No. And, I'm afraid I didn't think to ask. You see, I was a little preoccupied.

All I wanted was to forget the past and have a good time.'

'So you propositioned a young, attractive man . . . '

'No! It was nothing like that. He was looking as gloomy as I felt. We got to talking over a glass of iced tea. He said he knew the area well and would show me around. I said I would like that fine. We went for a long walk. It was fun and he was perfectly respectful. When I came down to dinner he was talking with Mr Armitage. They invited me to join them at their table.'

'Ah! So he knew Armitage?' The commissaire nodded his head wisely, then glanced up at the ceiling where there was a certain amount of muffled noise and groaning of floorboards.

'I don't think so. They just happened to be placed at the same table in the dining-room, I'm sure. They were both friendly and charming and it seemed a good idea to join them. It's not fun eating alone, especially when one is on holiday.'

Paul Dulac gave her a long, languid look, then pushed away from the table, leaving his dessert untouched.

'Excuse me, but I think there is something not right . . . '

'Perhaps it was something you ate,' Delphine said with what she hoped was a wicked sneer.

He wagged a finger at her and frowned in a comical manner.

'Gaston's mother would be offended to hear you say that. Her cuisine is legendary in the area.'

She watched him go, striding in long, easy steps into the hall. She heard the creak of his heavy tread on the bare wooden stairs, then the sound of his voice as he cursed loudly in French.

★   ★   ★

A minute went by, two, perhaps three, then two sets of footsteps sounded on the stairs and padded across the hall.

Delphine looked up to see Paul enter the room, followed by a somewhat dopey Gaston rubbing the back of his head and furiously blinking his eyes.

'Your nice, respectable English boy just tried to break Gaston's head.'

'What! I don't believe you! Where is he?'

Delphine was on her feet, straining her neck as though she expected to see Mark come sauntering into the room, all naïveté and innocence.

'He's gone. Vanished into the night.' He snapped his fingers and the report it made echoed in the high-ceilinged room. 'An efficient escape, non? Do you still believe, Delphine, that this Mark Easton of yours is nothing more than an innocent dupe?'

'Yes, I do!' Delphine hugged herself, shivering, partly in fear, partly because she was freezing, dressed as she was, half-naked and bare-footed. These old French farmhouses were built to keep the heat of the day out, but it was now halfway through the evening and cooling down.

'You are cold,' Paul said. 'I will get

Gaston to telephone his sister. She lives a few kilometres away. She is about your size and will be able to provide you with something more practical to wear.'

As Paul turned and conversed with Gaston, who was still looking shaken and unsteady on his feet, Delphine drew in a deep breath and let it out in a long, exasperated sigh.

She could well imagine what kind of wardrobe Gaston's sister would have. These people were simple country folk, isolated deep in the heart of the countryside. There was nothing for miles around but olive groves and lavender fields.

She wanted to tell the two men not to bother, that she would put up with the cold as long as Madame could provide a soft bed and plenty of clean blankets.

However, she said nothing and huddled by the dying embers of the fire, worrying about Mark and hoping he wasn't going to try anything heroic on her behalf. There had been no sound of a car engine, which meant he was still roaming around out there somewhere.

During supper Mark had intimated that Paul and Gaston were not exactly what they seemed and had given Delphine a whispered warning not to trust either of them. She had wanted to keep an open mind, but had ended up feeling more confused.

Certainly, Paul Dulac and his erstwhile sergeant had turned up out of the blue after the police inspector in charge of the murder case had warned her to stay in her hotel room until contacted.

She hadn't questioned the validity of Paul's identification, though now she thought about it, he seemed a bit too refined for the rôle of policeman. And Gaston was the complete opposite.

★ ★ ★

A knock on the outer door and a young, feminine voice talking and laughing with obvious pleasure, made

Delphine look up from her dark thoughts.

She stood up and moved nearer to the door into the hall where she could see Gaston and Paul standing with a young woman who was hanging around Paul's neck, giving him more than the customary greeting.

Paul's arms were around her shapely figure and her feet were off the ground as he swung her around.

I bet her toes are curled inside her shoes, Delphine thought with a slight uncomfortable flip of her heart. She cleared her throat loudly, not at all sorry to spoil their pleasure at seeing one another.

'Ah, Delphine!' Paul put the French-woman down and they came into the living-room together, but still attached at the hip, Delphine noticed. 'May I present Gaston's little sister, Maryse, who has brought you some clothes to wear.'

'Hello, mademoiselle.' Maryse smiled broadly and extended her hand in greeting. 'I speak English. Paul's my teacher. He's very good.'

'I'm sure he is — um — mademoiselle . . . '

'Maryse! I am called Maryse. And you are Delphine — ah! A French name! A pretty French name — a flower, non?'

As she was speaking, Maryse handed over the clothes she had brought. They were hardly what Delphine had expected. Instead of old-fashioned peasant wear, they were somewhere at the other end of the spectrum.

There was a white off-the-shoulder top, which was semi-transparent, and a multi-coloured floral gipsy skirt that was long, but was scooped up at one side and she wasn't sure she had the kind of thighs to show off in it.

The shoes, thankfully, were plain black leather slipperettes with rubber soles. And there was a heavy shawl in peacock blue with flowers and stars embroidered on it in gold silk threads, reminiscent of dancing, wild-eyed gipsies.

'Oh, and there is this.' Maryse

proffered a small pouch bag, bulging with a variety of contents. 'Personal, you understand.'

Delphine took a quick peek into the bag and smiled her gratitude for the toiletries she found there, including a few cosmetic items that were probably wholly unsuitable, and not Delphine's chosen colours, but she was thankful for them.

'Well, now everybody is happy,' Paul said.

Delphine noticed how his hand lingered on the French girl's shoulder in a possessive, intimate manner and she remembered how it had felt to have that same hand touching her own bare skin. She gave a shudder and hugged her new clothes to her more tightly.

'Oh, you have a cold, Delphine!' Maryse exclaimed, her eyes full of genuine concern. 'Paul, she has a cold. She must go to bed right away.'

As if she had been waiting for her cue, Madame Lacoste appeared, a long neck-to-ankle cotton nightdress in her hands, which she passed to Delphine and indicated for her to follow.

In her room, later, with the shutters closed tightly against the night and with Gaston mounting guard, Delphine listened to the sounds of jollity coming from the living-room where Maryse and Paul were enjoying each other's company.

6

Delphine had no idea how long she had been asleep. She must have drifted off even while thinking she could not possibly close her eyes. Because of the heavy shutters the room was as dark as could be. And the silence drummed in her ears.

Downstairs, the old grandfather clock continued its monotonous marking of time, and the old timbers of the house creaked from time to time, but there was no other sound. Even the crickets had bedded down for the night and nothing stirred.

Moving as carefully as she was able, Delphine felt about her, but there was no lamp and the tiny chink of silver grey light that squeezed in through a crack at the window, was not sufficient to allow her to see her watch.

Gradually, as her eyes became more

accustomed to the dark, she could make out shapes.

She distinguished the tall, bulky form of the wardrobe, the smaller, angular shape of a chair, and ahead was the door. She could feel a draught of cool air rushing through the gap at the bottom, chilling her bare toes as she shuffled towards it.

With her hand firmly clasping the knob, she started to turn it, surprised when the door opened, though it made a loud, metallic grating sound and gave an agonised shriek as it moved only a few inches.

The door wasn't the only thing to emit a shriek. Delphine did a fair imitation of it when a bright light was shone full in her face.

What's more, it came from inside the room rather than the corridor beyond.

'You are not thinking of leaving us, are you, Delphine?'

It was the voice of Paul Dulac that came to her through her thudding heart and singing ears. He lowered the torch slightly, which had been blinding her, and she blinked down into his striking face with its attractive, yet scornful smile.

'Have you been there all night?' Delphine's voice was small, weak and breathless.

'Of course. I came up shortly after midnight. You were sleeping like a baby.'

'There is absolutely no reason for you being inside my room!' She sounded a bit braver now, but she was still shaking all over like a jelly.

'Just doing my job, mademoiselle.'

'Don't you ever sleep? Anyway, I thought Gaston was posted outside.'

'Ah, oui! Poor Gaston. He had a little too much of his mother's famous wine and his head was hurting, thanks to your friend, so I decided to replace him.'

'But Gaston was *outside* my room!' Delphine was furious, but more at herself for being so ineffective, rather than at the detective.

'That is true, but I felt that I would serve you better by being in the room with you.'

He got to his feet stiffly and she realised he had been sitting on the floor. No wonder he looked tired.

Paul Dulac's long arm snaked out towards her and she jerked away, but he was simply reaching for the light switch. Suddenly the room was filled with uncertain, yellow light. He switched off his torch and smiled at her through a half-yawn.

'Well, Delphine? You have not yet told me what you had in mind when you opened this door.'

Delphine clenched her back teeth and thought quickly.

'I need to go to the bathroom seeing that there are no en suite facilities here.'

His face cracked open into a wide grin, showing strong, square and even white teeth. It was a good-looking face, Delphine thought, even though there was a touch of hardness there.

Such a pity that he was so . . . so

what? Insufferable? Obnoxious?

They were adjectives she had used on more than one occasion about past men in her life. She wasn't sure she could use the same labels for Paul Dulac. In fact, she wasn't sure of anything any more.

'I apologise,' Paul said, giving her a mock bow. 'Please go to the bathroom. I cannot see you going much farther in that nightdress.'

She saw the twinkle of amusement in his eyes and suddenly remembered, with a pink flush to her cheeks, that she was wearing Madame Lacoste's voluminous cotton nightdress.

'Really!' Delphine frowned and gathered folds of material together in front of her before stepping past him into the corridor outside.

Feeling completely disorientated, she turned to the left without thinking. Paul Dulac cleared his throat and tapped her on the shoulder, making her jump afresh.

'It's that way,' he said, pointing to the

right. 'Third floor on the left. There is no lock, but I will make sure that you are safe.'

'As long as you do it from outside,' Delphine told him through gritted teeth.

After a few minutes of sitting there in the cold, blue-painted bathroom with its ancient facilities and the smell of disinfectant, Delphine prepared to face her French gaoler again.

She really was in a pickle, she thought. It was too much for a simple English girl who only came on holiday to have a good time.

'Delphine!'

She looked up sharply at the sound of her name, which seemed to be coming from outside and somewhere above her.

There was a scratching sound and something pinged as the high, frosted glass window set in the wall above the toilet swung open and a face appeared.

'Mark!' Delphine hissed out his name, looking desperately at the door in case Paul Dulac was out there with his ear against the wooden panel. 'What on earth . . . ?'

'Ssh!' Mark put a finger to his lips and frowned down at the nightdress. 'Good lord, what's that tent you're wearing?'

'It's Madame Lacoste's night attire for unexpected guests,' she whispered back at him.

'Well, it's going to make things a little difficult, but we haven't any choice.' He swivelled his head and looked behind him, then he was halfway through the window, holding out his hands to her. 'Come on. You'll have to climb up on the loo seat and for heaven's sake don't fall in.'

'Then what?'

'Don't ask questions, Delphine. Just do as I say.'

'But I can't . . . '

'Look, I'm risking life and limb to rescue you.'

'But what about . . . ?'

'Delphine, do you trust me or not?'

She stared up at him and nodded slowly.

'Yes. As a matter of fact, I do.'

'Well, don't sound so reluctant to admit it. Now — get up on the seat and climb out of this window. Don't worry. I won't let you fall.'

Delphine only took seconds to think about it, then she yanked up the nightdress and tied it loosely around her hips.

She stepped up on the toilet seat and wobbled precariously, but Mark grabbed for her hands, steadying her.

Suddenly, there was a loud rapping noise on the door and Paul Dulac was calling out her name.

'Sorry!' she called back to him. 'I'll only be a minute.'

An exasperated sigh reached her and she held her breath, her heart pounding against her chest wall and up into her throat.

'Good girl!' Mark was full of admiration as he hauled her through the window and on to the corrugated tiled roof of a small outbuilding.

'Oh, dear!' Delphine looked about her and wondered how she was ever going to get down from there. 'I hate heights, you know. This is awful.'

Mark hugged her tightly to him and planted a warm kiss on her temple, then he was leading her gently but firmly down to the edge of the roof.

'Worst part's over,' he assured her as he lowered himself on to an ancient, rustic ladder that must have served generations of Lacostes since the Revolution. 'Turn round, Delphine, and come down the ladder backwards. Grip hold of the sides as soon as they're within reach. I'll guide you from behind.'

At that precise moment, Delphine missed her footing on the first rung of the ladder and ended up slithering to the bottom, narrowly missing Mark's head on the way.

'Oh, dear, I'm sorry!'

'Well, that's one way to come down a ladder, but it's not to be recommended.

Here, give me your hand. Pity about the bare feet. The ground's pretty rough and stony around here.'

With one hand hanging on to her nightdress and the other clasped in Mark's, Delphine managed to get her legs working, even though she could see precious little.

'Where are we going?'

She winced as sharp blades of dried grass jabbed at her naked soles.

'Save your breath until we get there. Come on. Put a spurt on. That Frenchman is no doubt beating down the bathroom door by now.'

*   *   *

Mark was just as breathless as she was as they ran along a rough track and skidded around a corner where the first lavender field was. Delphine felt the rough brush of the aromatic herb against her bare legs.

Come to think of it, why was she so relieved to get away from what was supposed to be a safe house?

She had been placed in protective custody, for her own good, and here she was running away from it. She must be crazy. Either that or something was badly wrong here.

'Is that your car?' she gasped as she made out the outline of the beetle-shaped VW parked just ahead of the trees.

'That's my baby, yes.'

'So that's why we didn't hear the engine start up. You had left it here and . . . '

'And walked — yes. Of course! I'm not stupid, though I may look it.'

'I don't think you look at all stupid, Mark,' Delphine said warmly.

She didn't know any other man who would have gone to such lengths to help her, given her same circumstances. They had all been either wimps or bullies, not a hero among them.

And here was Mark, a man she hardly knew, risking all sorts of trouble in order to rescue her.

'Consider yourself rescued, Delphine,' Mark said on cue, as if he had read her mind.

He opened the car door and saw her safely into the passenger seat, then climbed in behind the wheel. He put the key in the ignition, but before he did anything else he leaned over to her, took hold of her chin and planted a not too brotherly kiss on her lips.

'Oh!' Delphine blinked at him through the darkness. The kiss had stirred up a few butterflies that belonged to excitement rather than fear.

'I hope you don't mind, but I've been longing to do that since the moment I laid eyes on you.' Mark stared at her with big, hungry eyes, then looked away bashfully like a shy schoolboy on his first date.

'I don't mind at all,' she told him. 'In fact, I rather liked it and, to be quite honest, I needed something just like that. But Mark, please tell me — why did you feel it necessary to rescue me? I mean — why rescue? Commissaire Dulac and his sergeant were supposed to be looking after me, keeping me safe from whoever killed that man in the alley. Some mafia boss, apparently. I was a witness and . . . '

Mark was staring at her again, but this time his eyes were closed to narrow slits as he listened to what she was saying.

'Mafia?'

Delphine hesitated, chewing on her lips.

'You know, Mark, the more I think about it the more ridiculous the whole thing becomes. After all, this kind of thing doesn't happen to real people, does it? I mean — it's total Hollywood!'

'Cloud Cuckoo Land, I'd say,' Mark played with a tendril of her hair, wrapping it round and round his finger.

Delphine gave a delicious shudder, then realised that she was also shivering because she was cold and her borrowed nightie clung damply to her perspiring, but rapidly-cooling skin.

'Let's get you out of here.' But still Mark's hands lingered around her face and shoulder. 'Delphine, I don't know what you've got yourself into, but those men back there aren't with the police.'

'They're not?' she almost yelled and Mark held up a cell phone.

'I checked. The local gendarmes have never heard of Commissaire Paul Dulac — so tit for tat, you might say.'

Delphine's eyes were large as she tried to take in what he was saying.

'What? But he has an identity card and — and he shot Mr Armitage who had a knife and was going to kill me, and . . . '

Mark's face paled visibly in the dim light.

'Oh, God, Delphine! Harry Armitage was my uncle.'

'But . . . '

Mark shrugged. 'I hardly knew him. He paid for me to come to France. Just before you turned up we had had a flaming row. He wanted me to take over the family business. I didn't feel ready for that kind of commitment. He did the usual guilt bit. You know, 'You're no nephew of mine, Mark!' '

Mark shook his head sadly and turned the key in the ignition. The car coughed asthmatically, but failed to start. He tried again, his forehead creasing. Nothing. He swore softly, then a small sound made them both look up.

Through the windscreen a tall, powerful figure was silhouetted.

Paul Dulac had a pistol held steadily in both hands and it was pointing directly at them. He was smiling coldly.

7

Delphine could hear Paul Dulac's raised voice in the next room where he was ensconced with Mark. It sounded as though poor Mark was being put through a rigorous third-degree questioning routine.

'What's happening?'

She turned on Gaston as her anger rose, but it was to no avail.

The sergeant — or whatever he really was — could not speak sufficient English and made as if he could not understand her rough, schoolgirl French either. She was wasting her time trying to get anything out of him.

Madame Lacoste came in once and stared hard at Delphine. There followed a heated few words between mother and son, then the old woman threw up her hands and went out to see to the livestock, a bucket full of grain in one hand and a wicker basket in the other to collect any eggs that had been laid in the night. It was six-thirty in the morning and none of them had had any sleep.

★ ★ ★

Finally, the door opened and Mark came in, looking a bit shaken and not too well pleased by the situation in which he found himself.

'Are you all right?' Delphine asked, jumping to her feet and taking his arm to lead him to a chair beside hers. 'Did that brute beat you?'

'Not exactly, but he might as well have done,' Mark said, sitting down heavily and looking as though he could happily keel over at any given moment. 'I don't know what his game is, Delphine, but don't trust him.'

'I never did!' Delphine heard herself saying and received a quizzical look from the big Frenchman that made her shudder and blink back at him like a scared rabbit.

'You are a fool to believe what this idiot tells you!' Paul ground out the words angrily, his eyes flashing like black diamonds.

'I believed what you told me,' she retaliated sharply, feeling a sudden surge of bravado. 'And look where that got me.'

'You are alive, are you not? What more could you ask at this moment?'

'I have plenty to ask. I would like to know why I can't just be put on a plane back to England.'

Delphine drew in a short breath. 'I want to go home.'

'You do not know the people with whom you are dealing.'

'That's certainly true. I took you to be an honest policeman, but you're not, are you?'

Mark grabbed her wrist and she winced as he held on tightly.

'Delphine — no!'

Paul Dulac moved forward and rested his weight on his hands. His face, with its stubborn chin showing a dark, blue-black shadow, jutted forward menacingly.

'What have you been telling her? What fantasies have you been weaving about me?'

Mark shook his head and tried to pass it off with an embarrassed laugh.

'I never met you before now. How could I tell her anything?'

Delphine started to protest, but Mark jerked brutally on her wrist and she realised that he meant for her to keep quiet.

She quickly swallowed the words that had formed in her throat and clamped her mouth shut. Her mother had always told her how open and gullible she was.

For the first time, she realised that the woman had been right. Delphine had gone through life accepting everything and everyone on face value, trusting everyone, wearing her heart on her sleeve.

'Mark didn't tell me anything,' she lied and felt a flush of guilt creep up from the base of her neck.

Paul Dulac's eyes, however, were not so much on her face as on her body. It seemed that he had only just noticed how she was dressed and was greedily drinking it all in.

The voluminous nightgown had gone, replaced by the skirt and top provided for her by Gaston's sister. Delphine knew that she must look like a gipsy girl who had outgrown her clothes.

'What are you going to do with us?' Delphine asked, glad that Mark had released her wrist and was now encircling her waist in a manner that both comforted and reassured her.

Paul put a foot up on a chair, leaned an elbow on his knee and stroked his chin reflectively. He took a maddeningly long time to reply to her question.

'Well — I am not at all sure that I will do anything with your little boyfriend here,' he said slowly, his gaze shifting lazily in Mark's direction. 'After all, I am only being paid to protect you, Delphine.'

'Then do your job, but Mark is with

me, so he's part of the deal.'

'Ha! A package deal — like a holiday. But suppose I do not want to do anything for Mark? He did not see the murder. My orders were to protect one witness — Mademoiselle Delphine Harvey. We were not told that you came with — how do you say — excess baggage.'

'He is not excess baggage!' Delphine objected, feeling suddenly hot and claustrophobic in the tight circle of Mark's arm. 'He's a very nice person and he only wanted to help me. It's not his fault that he's now implicated by association. If you're what you say you are — Commissaire Dulac — you will put us both under police protection, but preferably in some place that has more home comforts.'

Paul's smile was slow and tinged with ice.

'To criticise the home of your generous hostess is impolite, Delphine. Your being here could well put Madame Lacoste at risk. She lives here

69

alone, except when Gaston is on leave.'

Delphine looked out of the window and saw the bent figure of the Frenchwoman surrounded by clucking chickens and honking geese.

She was old and quite ugly with her dried parchment skin pleated like a concertina. But she did not strike Delphine as being wicked.

She looked back at Paul, but the anger and the fear she felt because of him was still there.

'Just who are you, really?'

'I told you. I am who and what it says on my identity card. Why can't you believe me?'

'Because she's no fool, Dulac!'

Mark pulled himself up to his feet and the two men faced one another across the table like a couple of gunslingers of the old Wild West.

'What if Delphine chooses not to follow through on this protection bit, eh? What then? If you're truly what you say you are, we can walk out of here right now and you can't do a thing to stop us.'

'Delphine is a witness to a serious crime and because she saw what she saw and the killer saw her, her life now is in danger.' Paul's fists were clenching and unclenching. 'Can't you see that?'

'Your method of protection leaves a lot to be desired, Dulac! Being in protective custody is one thing, but you are treating us like prisoners.'

'You, I can let go any time, but do not tell me how to deal with a hostile witness who doesn't have the sense to act in her own interests.'

Mark had become beetroot to the roots of his hair and Delphine could see a pulse beating rapidly in his neck.

He moved closer to her, his eyes still on the Frenchman and once more he was gripping her wrist, urging her to go with him.

'Come on, Delphine. We're getting out of here.'

He pushed against her until she nearly overbalanced and her feet were forced to step out. Gaston was closing in, fingering the pistol he wore in a holster beneath his armpit. Paul stood calm and silent, waiting.

'Where do you think you are taking her?' he said at last when they were almost out of the room.

'I don't know, but we'll find somewhere. She'll be all right.' Mark turned his red face to her. 'Don't worry, Delphine. I'll look after you. You'll be safe with me.'

Delphine tried to smile back gratefully at him, but her lips wobbled too much. She opened her mouth to speak, and that was when Paul Dulac made his move.

*   *   *

It all happened so quickly she thought she had imagined it. Suddenly she was pulled to one side. A well-aimed fist wafted by her cheek and connected with Mark's jaw with a dull thud.

Mark keeled over, an expression of incredulity frozen on his face. His eyes were still open when he hit the opposite wall and slid down it, first to a sitting position on the floor, then crumpled over like a rag doll with the stuffing knocked out of it.

Delphine ran to him, full of concern. She was already on her knees beside him, when Paul grabbed her from behind and hauled her to her feet.

'Gaston!' Paul barked out an order to his colleague while he wrestled with Delphine, who was kicking and fighting him for all she was worth, even though she knew she didn't stand a chance of getting away.

Gaston heaved Mark up and dragged him backwards out into the hall, the heels of his trainers squeaking over the tiled floor, his comatose head lolling helplessly.

'You monster!'

Delphine's heel found Paul's foot and she stamped down hard, though the soft leather slipperettes she was wearing hardly made him wince.

'Please, Delphine.'

He turned her around to face him, but still kept a strong grip on her upper arms. He shook her so hard that her teeth rattled.

'You must stop this behaviour or you will end up like your boyfriend there.'

'Will you please stop referring to him as my boyfriend!'

She stamped her foot with renewed fury, then sank inside herself, weak with frustration.

'But I thought that he was just that — or at least . . . ' Paul grinned suddenly. ' . . . at least someone you would like to have as your boyfriend.'

'Don't be ridiculous. I hardly know him.'

There was a slight hesitation before he spoke again.

'How long does it take for two people to fall in love, Delphine?'

She wished he wouldn't keep saying her name like that. She had never liked her name much, but coming from his lips it sounded so different and, well, beautiful.

'I am not in love with Mark Easton,' she informed him firmly. 'For your information, I am not in love with anybody. I'm finished with falling in love. It always brings me more trouble than I can handle.'

'Like right now, do you mean?'

'Ooh! You are so — so . . . ' Lost for words, Delphine sank even lower as though her bones had suddenly become disengaged and free-floating.

'Perhaps, Delphine, you fall in love with the wrong men.'

'Are there any right ones? I'm beginning to doubt it.'

He laughed softly and his breath wafted the hair on the top of her head, which gave her a quick sprinkling of gooseflesh like icy fingers playing up and down her spine.

'Ah, the words of a woman spurned.'

'Certainly not!'

'I see. Heaven forbid that any man should spurn you. Is that it?'

'No man has ever spurned me. I'm always the first to break off relations.'

'So! Not spurned. Burned, maybe? That, they tell me, is much worse.'

Delphine groaned. 'You're impossible, do you know that?'

'I have been called worse names, I assure you.'

'By woman you've burned no doubt?'

'Only the ones who thought they could change me.'

He was bending his head and looking so deeply into her eyes that Delphine felt oddly hypnotised by this anti-hero who didn't seem at all real, but who had a great impact on her confused hormones.

'Didn't your mother tell you that it's rude to stare?' she asked flippantly.

The corner of his mouth lifted into a half-smile.

'It was my mother who taught me how to do it.'

Delphine gave him what she hoped would pass for a derogatory sneer and tried to pull away from him, but he held on fast to her.

'Let me go!'

'Delphine, if I was not a policeman on duty I think I might want to kiss you right now.'

'But you're not a policeman, are you?' Too late she realised the implication that might be read into her hasty words.

'Is that what you want to believe? So, if I kiss you there's no problem, is there, Delphine?'

'Don't you dare!'

Her mouth hadn't closed over her words when his mouth claimed hers in a kiss that ripped all the breath and all the fight out of her in just a few terrifyingly blissful seconds. The world tipped, swayed and burst into stars all around her before she was finally able to put her emotions on hold.

8

Of course it was not love that she felt for Paul Dulac. It was some kind of fatal attraction, an affliction. There should be a treatment for it, she thought, like locking his type up where no innocent woman could fall foul of his charms.

Mark Easton was much more her kind of man. He wasn't tough, although he had proved to be some kind of hero with the way he tried to help her in the face of unknown danger. It wasn't his fault that the Frenchman was stronger and more ruthless.

Right from the start, Delphine had been aware of a gnawing at her insides that she couldn't put a label on. It had hit her the moment Paul walked into the hotel and presented himself as her protector.

And she had believed him. Just like

that! Some protector he had turned out to be, murdering a poor, defenceless old man and beating up his nephew who had simply got in the way.

And it wouldn't take much to make him treat her badly either, she thought, rubbing the red weals on her arms where his fingers had dug in so viciously.

'You bruise easily,' Paul said as though he had read her mind. 'I must be more careful how I handle you. I am not used to being with fragile English maidens.'

Delphine suppressed a shudder. 'What are you going to do with us?'

'It is not my decision. I am paid to follow orders.'

'And your orders are to railroad two innocent people out of their hotel and keep them prisoner in — in this . . . '

Her hands and her eyes swept the room and his eyes followed, the hint of a smile breaking out on his face.

'It is rustique,' he said. 'But then, they are poor people. Not everybody in

Provence is rich, you know, Delphine. A lot of these families have their roots going back a lot further than the influx of English and American tourists draped with jewellery and throwing money away as if it meant nothing at all.'

'I realise that this isn't what you might call the beautiful people belt, but . . . '

'But it is beautiful, non?'

He was standing by the open window. The warm breeze was wafting in, carrying with it the perfume of the lavender fields.

Delphine went to stand beside him and looked out at a sea of purple waves and patches of dark green where the fields left off and the olive groves began.

'Oh, yes, it's beautiful,' she agreed and caught her breath as he turned and looked down at her, his eyes gazing so deeply into hers that it was like a physical experience.

She wanted to turn away, walk away,

run. All she could do was stand there and wait and wonder, feeling scared and excited all at once.

Nothing happened. A small crease appeared on Paul's forehead. He jerked away from her as if something had just occurred to him that he didn't like.

'Don't worry, Delphine. Nothing bad will happen to you while you are in my charge, neither you nor your friend — your knight in shining armour, as you no doubt think of him.'

'I'm not that stupid!'

'No?' He was striding away from her, looking out into the hall, his head swivelling from right to left. 'Madame Lacoste!'

'Oui!' came back from the nether regions of the house and Madame Lacoste's feet scuffed the floor as she approached.

There was a muttered conversation that Delphine couldn't quite follow, but she guessed he was organising lunch. What she didn't expect was the old lady appearing a few minutes later with a large wicker basket covered by a chequered cloth.

The woman wore a big smile and said something about Gaston, but Paul shook his head, thanked her and took the basket from her.

'You need to get out and breathe some fresh air,' he said, turning to Delphine. 'I thought you might appreciate a picnic. The day is hot, but I know a good place.'

'What about Mark.'

'What about him?'

'Is he coming?'

'No. I do not trust him. Gaston will stay here with him.'

'There's nothing wrong with Mark. He's a perfectly ordinary, nice person who's only trying to help me.'

There was a short silence and she could almost imagine the whirring of the Frenchman's brain as he chewed on her words.

He transferred the picnic basket to his other hand, and held one hand out to her in invitation.

'Do you want to come with me or not? If it is so abhorrent to you to share a picnic outside, then you must say. We can eat lunch here at the table with the others. It is the day when the field workers come. They are mostly old men with old, traditional habits. They tear the bread with their hands and dip it in their wine because most of them have no teeth. They have been working hard in the fields and sometimes they do not wash too regularly.'

'I'll come with you,' Delphine told him quickly and the smile that had been playing about his mouth all morning came to fruition, lighting up his whole face. 'But I warn you, if you lay a finger on me, Commissaire Dulac, you will live to regret it.'

He gave a short, but cheerful laugh, showing startling white teeth against the golden brown of his tanned skin.

'I'm not sure that either of us would regret it, Delphine, but since you are so afraid of me I will behave myself — for now. After all, I am a policeman on duty.'

'So you say!'

'You have no other option but to believe me. At least, unlike your friend, Mark, I do have an identity card.'

Again he held out his hand to her.

'Come. It is a shame to waste those new clothes on these four walls and a lot of old men.'

She frowned at him, then was immediately aware of his appreciative gaze travelling down the whole length of her.

'They're not my clothes,' she reminded him and he nodded.

'No, but they look far more attractive on you than on Maryse. You should always wear things like that — bright and cheerful to go with your personality.'

Delphine ignored his hand and swept out of the house in front of him.

'You know nothing about my personality.'

9

Maybe it had just been a throwaway line to win her over, calling her bright and cheerful. She had been that once, but life had pulled her around the edge lately and right now she was hardly in a situation that would make anybody's morale perk up.

'That is where you are wrong.' Delphine had been striding ahead, not really knowing where she was going, but felt the need to keep moving. Paul grabbed her wrist and pulled her around so that she was facing in the opposite direction.

'We go this way. Your sense of direction leaves a lot to be desired, Delphine.'

'What makes you think you're such an expert in judging people?' she asked, rather than keep up an uncomfortable silence.

Paul had veered off to the right, taking an almost unrecognisable path through the nearest field of lavender.

★　★　★

As the tall, flowering fronds of each bush grazed her legs as they walked, Delphine breathed in the heady aroma and immediately relaxed.

'I don't know that I'm an expert,' Paul was saying, walking slightly ahead of her because there was no room to walk side by side. 'Before I joined the police, I did a course in psychology. I was always interested in people and what motivated them. There is the genetic thing, of course, but I work on the basis that all people are born equal and innocent. It's what happens to them in life that shapes them, inside and out.'

'I wonder what shaped you, then,' Delphine mused out loud and he gave a low chuckle, but ignored her remark.

'For example, take Gaston's mother.

You wouldn't believe that she was once a beautiful young girl, would you?'

'That,' Delphine grimaced, 'is asking a little too much, but I suppose she might have been pretty once — about a hundred years ago.'

'She was beautiful, believe me. I've seen her wedding photographs taken forty years ago.'

'What happened?'

'Hard work, poverty — especially after her husband died, leaving her with five children to raise single-handed. Ill health took her looks and the sun and the wind did the rest. When Gaston joined the police force it was the proudest moment of her life. Unfortunately, he does not share her pride. He does not earn sufficient money to pay for his love of fast cars.'

'And fast women, no doubt?'

Another laugh.

'I do not enter into the private life of my associate. I know he dreams of owning a boat one day so he can sail around Cannes and Nice. It is his greatest passion.'

'Well, it's nice to have a passion of one sort or another.'

He grabbed her and swung her around so suddenly that she almost toppled over.

'And what is your passion, Delphine? Do you have one?'

'You're such an expert, why don't you find out for yourself?'

She pulled away from him and marched ahead for a while, chastising herself for being so provocative, for that's what she had been. Damn him! What was it about Paul Dulac that brought out the worst in her?

He made her feel like a wanton woman and part of her liked it, as if it was a secret side of her that had lain hidden all her life.

'Keep going straight ahead,' Paul called out a couple of minutes later as she stopped and wondered which of the three branches of the path to take. 'Head towards that small grove of olive trees. There's shade there — and a stream.'

They couldn't have found a more idyllic spot for a picnic, Delphine decided when she saw the gurgling stream sparkling like liquid diamonds as it rushed along between trees and boulders and mossy banks.

As the sun rose overhead the day had become much hotter, but here the sun was dappled as it filtered through the dark olive leaves.

'Oh, this is lovely!' she exclaimed breathlessly and couldn't keep the smile of delight from spreading all over her face.

'I am glad you like it,' Paul said, lowering the basket to a flat-topped rock which seemed as if it had been created especially to form a picnic table. 'Now, you take care of the table and the food while I do a bit of bird watching.'

'Bird watching!'

She had noticed the binoculars strung about his neck, but he didn't look any more like a bird watcher than he looked like a policeman.

He grinned down at her as she started taking things out of the basket.

'I want to make sure that we are alone,' he said and then threw back his head and laughed loudly at the shocked expression on her face.

'No, I am not going to seduce you, Delphine. I need to keep an eye out for unwanted visitors, that is all. You can never let your guard down for a minute.'

'Oh, that!' She heaved a sigh of relief and looked with interest at the food Madame had packed for them. Cured ham, strong brebis cheese from the Pyrénées, crusty bread, a selection of fruit and a bottle of wine were all set out on the tiny square of red and white chequered linen.

There weren't any plates and there appeared to be only one sharp knife, but there were, at least, two glasses, even though they were small tumblers of thick glass that looked antique.

'Ah!' Paul came back from surveying the surrounding terrain and, taking out a bottle opener from his pocket, opened the wine. 'Excellent. This, I guarantee, you will like.'

He poured some of the ruby red wine into the glasses and handed one to her. The heat of the day had warmed the wine to blood temperature and it smelled of fruit and the musky oak of the keg in which it had matured. Delphine took a tentative sip, remembering the roughhouse wine she had previously tasted. But this was not house wine.

'It's delicious,' she said as the wine flowed smoothly down her throat without burning.

She reached out and turned the bottle so she could read the label.

'Côtes du Roussillon '95,' Paul told her. 'It's one of my favourites.'

'You have good taste — at least in wine.' Delphine couldn't help the jibe, but he simply beamed at her and savoured the wine in his glass.

'I have good taste in many things, Delphine,' he said. 'Now, let's eat! I'm ravishing.'

'Yes, I suppose you are, in your way,' she dimpled, trying not to laugh at his faux pas, thinking that it wasn't such a great mistake — if he was whom he said he was.

10

The bullet went zinging between them, hitting the water and sending up a great dazzling spray. They had finished eating and were relaxing, lying back on their elbows, replete and tranquil, mainly because of the wine and the languid day that draped them like a warm blanket.

Suddenly, Paul was sprawling all over her, rolling with her, down the bank, into the stream. Then he was dragging her like a sack of wet coal up the farther bank where the trees were denser and gave more cover and the rocks were larger.

There was no need to ask what was happening. Someone was firing at them, probably at long range.

'Oh, God!' was all she could utter in a desperate whisper.

'Ça va?' he asked urgently, grasping

her shoulder. 'You are not hurt, Delphine?'

'No, no!' she told him, though she was having difficulty breathing because his weight was fully on her. 'Was that what I thought it was?'

'A bullet — yes! Keep your head down!'

Paul eased himself off her and that was when she noticed that he had his pistol in his hand.

That was also the moment when she stopped enjoying the intimacy of his body pressing down on hers and realised that this was no ploy to have his way with her.

This was the real thing. Somebody was definitely trying to kill one or both of them.

And Paul was definitely protecting her. It was time to reassess his position and hers.

Whatever she thought about him, it looked as though he was genuine when it came to what he did for a living.

He was indeed a commissaire in the

French police. And right now he was trying to save her life.

'Don't move!' Paul shouted at her, his big hand planted flatly on the centre of her chest, pushing her back into the rusty red earth as she tried to rise.

He got to his knees, then started to pull himself upright, the pistol held at the ready, his eyes scanning the horizon.

He looked so professional, so like something she had enjoyed watching on television, but even though this was the real thing, the whole situation had a dreamlike quality.

'Paul, be careful!' she called out to him and he turned to look at her, smiling.

That was when the second bullet zapped the air and found its target.

Paul gave a small cry as he was thrown backwards by the force of the bullet. She saw a spreading scarlet patch on his shirt.

'Paul!'

She let out a hoarse scream and threw herself at him without thinking.

'Little fool!' was all he could say and, encircling her with one arm, rolled again with her dizzily until they had reached lower ground.

'But you're hurt!' The words jerked out of her breathlessly.

'It is nothing! Don't move!'

They lay clasped in each other's arms for what seemed a long time. Delphine could feel Paul's heart beating against her and knew that her own heart was responding beat for beat.

She wished it was all over and done with. She wished it would never end.

'Oh, damn!' she muttered into his neck which was warm and smelled salty. 'They really do want to get rid of me, don't they?'

'Now she believes me!' Paul said with a grimace as she tried to shift her position. 'Keep still, will you! Do you want to get us both killed?'

★ ★ ★

How long they lay there like that was anybody's guess. It seemed like a very long time.

No other bullets strafed the place where they were.

Twice, three times, Delphine thought of suggesting that they try to make their escape, but she was reluctant.

She told herself that the would-be assassin was out there waiting for them to make a move. Maybe she was right.

'OK, Delphine,' Paul said eventually, his face crumpling in pain as he tried to move the arm where the shoulder had taken a bullet. 'One way or another, you've got to move!'

'I can't!' she breathed in his ear, fear paralysing her.

'You've got to! Everything I own has gone into cramp!'

'Oh! Sorry!'

Delphine shifted her position slightly. Nothing happened, except a flood of reluctance.

* * *

There were no more bullets.

She eased over a little more so that she was lying on the stony ground rather than on top of Paul.

'Mon Dieu! That's better!'

Delphine wasn't sure that it was better from her point of view, but she didn't want to be in the protection of a man who not only had a bullet in his shoulder, but who had cramp and might be rendered helpless at the wrong moment.

'Do you think he's gone?' she asked in a hoarse whisper, raising her head two inches so she could see across the vast purple lavender plain.

'How should I know?' Paul was pushing himself up into a sitting position, groaning slightly and rubbing his thighs with his good hand, while his left arm was hanging limply at his side.

'You're losing a lot of blood,' she said, noticing how far the red stain had spread already.

'So do something about it!'

He sounded angry, then he closed his eyes and gripped her hand.

Delphine looked down at Maryse's voluminous skirt and wondered what the Frenchwoman would have done in the circumstances.

She reached down and was able to tear two strips of material from around the hem of the skirt. With part of it, she staunched the bleeding wound.

With the rest, she manufactured a bandage and a sling.

The bullet had gone straight through Paul's shoulder, just beneath the collarbone. He had been so lucky.

There was the sound of a car engine starting up and driving off, fading into the distance. They could see the cloud of dust it created as it retreated from the scene.

'He's gone,' Paul said as Delphine finally helped him to his feet. 'I think we can go back to the farm now.'

* * *

It was a slow trudge to the farmhouse, where it sat squat among the lavender fields with its red pantile roof glowing in the afternoon sun.

The shabby old Breton spaniel was sufficiently roused to come running and barking as they drew near.

Paul was weak and leaning heavily on Delphine's shoulder. She could hear his laboured breathing and the odd grunt of pain as he stumbled along beside her.

It was strange how they had started out with him protecting her. Now the rôles seemed to be reversed.

'Gaston!' Delphine called out as soon as they were within hearing distance. 'Gaston, quick, help us!'

There was no sound or movement from the house. All that happened was that the dog barked louder and became more and more agitated, running around them in circles, its tail between its arthritic legs.

* * *

At last, a door opened and Madame appeared, shading her eyes from the glare of the sun.

She gave a gasp and came running forward, arms flailing the air, words flowing volubly from her toothless mouth.

'He's got a bullet in his shoulder,' Delphine shouted, knowing full well that the woman would not understand a word of it, but she couldn't think of any French at that moment and Paul was already sinking to his knees, his face ashen and his eyes closed.

Madame Lacoste pulled at Paul's good arm and tried to drag him towards the house.

'Where's Gaston?' Delphine yelled, though the woman was far from being deaf. 'Madame, où est Gaston?'

The woman looked distraught, then spun around as a couple of sleepy individuals came slowly out of the house, rubbing their eyes and scratching their sides.

'Henri, Georges! Ici, vite!'

Together the four of them managed to carry Paul into the living-room, where they laid him on an ancient, leather-covered horsehair sofa. Gaston's mother fetched a large, patchwork quilt and tucked him up, fussing about him like a mother hen.

She kept muttering to herself all the time as she fetched a bowl of warm water and began to bathe the bullet wound while one of the old men got on the phone and called the emergency medical services.

★ ★ ★

A few short hours later, Paul and Delphine walked out of the hospital and looked for a taxi.

He had recovered consciousness almost immediately and insisted on Delphine accompanying him to the hospital, saying she would be safer there with him than left on her own at the house.

'I can't understand why you're doing this, Paul,' Delphine said, shaking her head. 'You've had a bullet through your shoulder, for heaven's sake. The doctor said you should rest in hospital for a couple of days.'

'Bah! What does he know?'

'Well, I think he knows enough, being as how he's a surgeon. You really shouldn't have discharged yourself like that.'

'I'm all right, Delphine. Stop worrying. You are worse than my mother.'

'Do you really have a mother?'

He frowned darkly at her, then twisted his face into a wry smile.

'Even policemen have mothers, Delphine.'

'You surprise me. I thought maybe you were created on a computer that's affected by some terrible virus.'

'Thank you. I love you, too.'

'Well, isn't that a laugh!'

Delphine looked away so that he didn't catch the troubled look in her eyes.

That's when she saw Gaston making his way towards them, his face awash with anxiety.

When he caught up with them it was obvious that his anger was even stronger than the anxiety and, perhaps, tinged with a little guilt.

He should not have gone down into the town, leaving them wide open to attack. It was as much his fault as anybody's that Paul had been shot.

Paul clapped the younger detective on the back and pushed him towards the old banged up car that Gaston used when he was on leave.

It was an ancient Citroën Diane in faded beige and about the only thing that was still going strong was the engine.

There was a rapid trade-off of news, then Paul turned to Delphine to give her a translation. The way he moved in his seat told her that he was in considerable pain, despite the strong painkillers pumped into him at the hospital.

'He cannot forgive himself for leaving

us to our own devices.'

'I should think not,' Delphine said, giving Gaston a reprimanding look and making it as sharp as she could manage. 'I suppose he was on duty, too. I hope he has a good excuse for leaving his post.'

'He went to see his girl. There have been problems.'

Delphine clenched her teeth to prevent her from saying something she might regret later on.

She could see a muscle in Gaston's cheek twitching madly as he started up the car. He didn't once take his attention from the road ahead all the way back to the farmhouse.

The man was certainly bothered about something, but she wasn't totally convinced that it was the bullet in Paul's shoulder that had, undoubtedly, been meant for her.

11

Mark was the most pathetic, most miserable-looking character she had ever seen. Somehow, he had been totally forgotten in the rush to get Paul to hospital. She hadn't even asked where he was, so panicky was she that the Frenchman might die from his wound. Fortunately, the bullet had gone right through, as she had thought, and had done amazingly little damage.

The assurance given her by the surgeon was a great relief, though it was obvious that Paul should have stayed in hospital. He must be as strong as an ox, Delphine decided, to walk away from a wound like that, despite the fact that it was not life-threatening.

'I suppose you think I enjoy being trussed up like a pig for market and being left to my own devices for hours!'

Mark was struggling to sit up in his

narrow bed where he had been tied hand and foot by Gaston to stop him making another bolt for it.

Delphine tried not to smile as she pulled at the last cords that bound his ankles.

It really wasn't funny. Not in the slightest. But Mark did look so much like a pouty-mouthed little boy who had been thoroughly reprimanded, then forgotten, locked away alone in his room.

'I'll speak to Gaston about this later.' Paul was leaning heavily against the doorjamb, holding the arm that was in a sling close to his midriff. He was still pale, but some colour was returning to his cheeks.

'I can't believe that the French police treat people so abominably,' Delphine said, but she couldn't get the right tone of anger into her voice. He had saved her life, after all, and was undoubtedly hurting pretty badly.

Paul shook his head and shifted his position from one foot to another.

'We don't, normally, but then we don't deal with the American mafiosi every day. It was just unfortunate that the killing happened on my doorstep and that you were there to witness it.'

'But to tie poor Mark up like that . . . '

'As I've said — I'll speak with him. Gaston tends to get carried away at times and just lately — well, he's been a touch on the neurotic side. Woman trouble can do that to a man, you know.'

'No, I wouldn't know.'

She answered him sharply and went to stare out of the window where the sky was a dark navy blue and full of stars winking and twinkling and the hazy swathe of the Milky Way was clearly seen spanning the heavens.

'I was married once,' Paul said, the words coming out of the blue after a moment's silence. Then he waited, obviously wanting her to respond.

'What happened?' she asked.

'She could not stand being a

policeman's wife. We were together for two years before she divorced me. I swore I would give up my job, if I ever again met another woman who meant enough to me.'

'How would you know? Do you ever stay in one place long enough to find out?'

Why on earth was her heart throbbing and tripping over itself, just because he had told her, more or less, that he was not married? What difference did it make to her or their relationship, such as it was? He had already told her that he wasn't available.

'I think I will know. Anyway, this is my last case. As soon as I can hand you over safe and sound, I plan to retire to my farm.'

'Oh?'

Did that mean he had already found himself a woman worth giving up his job for? 'You have a farm?'

'Uh-huh. Not large. We grow herbs and fruit and organic vegetables.'

'No lavender fields?' she asked, noting he had said, 'We'!

He laughed softly and she was aware that he was very close behind her as she held on tightly to the windowsill.

Delphine sighed deeply.

She couldn't help it. She had a mental picture of Paul, long after she had returned to her home in Scotland, wandering about his farm with a pretty young wife on his arm and children laughing as they romped about, brown and healthy under the Provence sun.

Then she gave herself a little mental shake. What a laugh. His farm was probably no better than this old place — run down, creaking timbers that were alive with the local wildlife, chickens in the kitchen and preserves maturing overhead and in every foul-smelling cupboard. Well, it would take a real French countrywoman to appreciate that type of living.

'I'm sorry I'm keeping you from your retirement dream,' she said dryly.

'I have no regrets,' he said. 'Why should you?'

12

'Delphine! Delphine, wake up!' The urgent whisper and the tugging at her shoulder made Delphine wake with a start, her heart palpitating.

'Mark!' She couldn't believe her eyes and rubbed frantically at them to remove the last vestiges of sleep, thinking that maybe she was having a dream. 'What are you doing in my room?'

'Ssh! Keep your voice down.' He sat on the edge of her bed and took her hand. 'Gaston fell asleep outside my room. I was supposed to be locked in but the lock's faulty. At least he didn't tie me up this time.'

'But . . .'

'It's OK. Your handsome Frenchman is downstairs on the sofa, dead to the world. I guess whatever they gave him at the hospital is still working to keep him quiet.'

'Not to mention a bullet through his shoulder!'

'Yes . . . ' Mark looked down at her hand that lay in his and stroked the back of it with his thumb. 'I owe you an apology, Delphine.'

'What on earth for? Getting yourself hogtied?'

'Not that — no.'

He shifted about restlessly on the bed and the old springs creaked and twanged.

'What is it, Mark?' Delphine pulled herself up into a sitting position and reached out to touch his face with her fingertips.

He grabbed hold of her hand and pressed his lips to her palm. It gave her a warm, tender feeling towards him.

'I was wrong about Paul Dulac — no, I knew all along that he was the genuine article. The fact is, I was doing some sleuthing on my own behalf and — well, you got involved and while I regretted that, I — um . . . '

'Go on, Mark.'

'First of all, I want you to know what I — I'm very fond of you, Delphine, and I wouldn't do anything at all to hurt you.'

'What on earth are you talking about?'

Mark was staring at her with wide, naked eyes and she experienced a sudden surge of fear running like a cold finger up and down her spine.

'I told you the truth about Mr Armitage. He is — was — my uncle, and he did want me to take over the family business. The trouble was, I had reason to believe that he was mixed up in business that had a lot to do with a very different 'family'.

'He was in the States more than he was in England. We hardly ever saw him, yet when he was there he couldn't have been nicer. My aunt couldn't have children, so I was all set to inherit — well, whatever there was to inherit.'

'Well, that's nice — isn't it?'

'You don't understand, Delphine. The argument we were having when you walked in on us was not about the family inheritance, but the fact that he wanted me to take over from him — you know, what he was doing for his American bosses.'

He gave a sudden gulp and seemed unable to go on. Delphine gave his hand an encouraging squeeze.

'He was employed by a man who was, by any other name, a godfather. My uncle was a sick man. He had one task left to him before he retired — to kill . . . '

Delphine's hand rushed to her mouth and pressed down tightly to prevent her from crying out as she realised the truth behind Mark's words.

'He — he was a professional assassin?'

Mark shrugged.

'Something like that. He took ill on the night he was supposed to carry out the last — execution. Cancer was eating him away. He asked me to do it for him. I refused. Before we knew where we were, Tony Borgheza had done it for himself.'

'And I saw him do it. Oh, my God, Mark!'

'I guess we're both targets now. Maybe we always were. I believe that Commissaire Dulac is in their pay. It was something my uncle said when he was rambling in his sleep and under the influence of morphine. Something about that damned policeman Borgheza had dragged on to their side.'

'Oh, no!' Delphine closed her eyes with a groan.

So, Paul Dulac wasn't so honest after all. Even though she had never believed he could mean anything to her other than a tiny, unbelievable holiday fantasy, she had not bargained for this kind of thing.

She had suspected him, at one stage, of not being all he pretended to be, but then he had saved her life, or so she thought, and she no longer wanted to believe anything bad of him.

'Get dressed, Delphine.' Mark was pulling at her, dragging her out of bed. 'This time we may have better luck.

Come on. Hurry up.'

He turned his back on her to give her some privacy. Delphine pulled on her clothes with trembling, clumsy fingers.

Downstairs, the old clock in the hall was ticking with hidden menace as it ate away the minutes. Outside, a summer storm was raging.

★   ★   ★

They crept as silently as possible down the rickety old stairs, keeping to the wall edge where the timbers were more securely fixed.

Outside the room where Mark had been held prisoner there was only an empty chair, but the door was closed, the key turned in the lock, and the house was as silent as the grave. Gaston must have given up and gone to his own room, or was back in town seeing his girl.

Only a faint red glow came from the dying embers of the open fire in the kitchen. Paul Dulac was stretched out on the sofa, breathing heavily.

He must have passed out under the influence of the drugs they had given him at the hospital, for one arm was flung out, hanging limply to the floor. In his hand, the fingers holding on to it loosely, was his pistol.

Delphine and Mark exchanged looks, then tiptoed softly to the outer door, easing the bolt.

The old dog was sleeping outside on the worn doormat. He raised his head and cocked a curious eyebrow at them, twitching his pink nose. However, he settled down again immediately Delphine stroked his tangled ears.

'Phew!'

Mark blew out his cheeks as they closed the door behind them, turning their faces into the storm as they stepped off the veranda and headed, not for the lavender fields, but for the small town of Pugnac, five miles away.

After a few minutes of tentatively walking as if on fragile eggshells, Mark gripped Delphine's hand and started off at a steady trot.

The wind and the rain whipped Delphine's skirt around her legs, causing her to trip and stumble. Except for the intermittent flashes of lightning, the night had become as dense as black cotton wool.

'Are you sure you know the way?' she called out breathlessly.

If he gave a reply she never heard it. Through a heavy rattle of thunder she heard a distinctive crack and Mark pitched forward, falling on his face and rolling over and over until a clump of wild thyme arrested his progress.

She stood looking at him, her mouth hanging open, her brain numb. He didn't move, didn't make any attempt to get up. It was almost as if he were dead.

Delphine was aware of a movement, rather than a sound, for it was impossible to hear anything above the loud soughing of the wind, the lashing of the rain and the booming of the thunder.

She looked sideways and drew in a fearful gasp as a large figure in silhouette loomed up on her right as a second pair of footsteps crunched gravel somewhere to the left.

Then a double flash of forked lightning lit up his face as he took a step towards her, the gun still in his hand, and pointing directly at her. And she could see in the Frenchman's grim face that he meant business. This time, however, there was no-one around to save her.

13

It was bizarre, Delphine thought, that in the most frightening moment of her life, when she was facing almost certain death, she felt calm and totally in control of her emotions.

The first thought that went through her head when she stared down the barrel of that mean-looking, very real pistol, was that they would never believe her back home when she told them the story of what happened when she decided to ditch her inhibitions and have a good time in the South of France.

Her second thought had been the regret she felt at never being able to see again the lavender fields and the olive groves. After that, she wondered what it would have been like to get to know Mark properly once he had sorted out the ugly business of his mafia connections with the French police. She would never know now.

As this last thought flashed through her mind she could see Mark lying, lifeless, only a yard or two on her right. If she turned her back on the gun in the Frenchman's hand she might be able to see the porch light of the old farmhouse.

She wondered if she dared do that, and if she did, would he pull the trigger and shoot her in the back? Could any man be that low?

Delphine's face suddenly crumpled as she whispered the name that her heart was forcing through her paralysed lips.

'Paul! Oh, Paul! Oh, dear God, no!'

The Frenchman moved in closer and she heard his low, throaty laugh. He had seemed so nice, so legitimate. She glanced once more in Mark's direction, but he still wasn't moving and looked like he would never move again.

'Move!' The pistol beckoned and a hand shot out and gripped her above the elbow in a painful, vice-like grip.

'Why?' She looked up into the mean face that had once seemed so normal, so friendly. 'Why are you doing this?'

★ ★ ★

Gaston Lacoste gave her a shrug and a toss of his big head. His face was streaming with rivulets of rain that dripped from his nose and his chin.

He hardly seemed aware of the discomfort. He tugged at her and she went with him, surprised to find that the plan was obviously not to kill her right away.

He muttered something in rapid, guttural French to her when he thought she wasn't moving as quickly as she might, but her feet in the thin leather slippers were slithering about in the mud and she could barely keep her footing.

'Is it the money, Gaston?' she asked, frantically trying to defuse the situation in any way she could.

It never occurred to her that he

couldn't understand what she was saying. 'It's not worth it, Gaston. It's not worth making yourself a murderer for money. They'll find you and put you in prison and then what will become of your dreams? What will your family think of you? Your poor mother?'

Gaston stopped in his tracks and she barged into him and would have fallen, but he braved himself and kept her upright.

'Woman! Be quiet!'

So, he did understand some English and, like most of the French population who were under the age of forty, he probably spoke quite a lot of it, too.

★ ★ ★

He didn't take her to the town, but to a broken-down barn where a car with darkened windows waited, silent and ominous. Gaston pushed her inside and left the big sliding door open. There was a flurry of startled doves above their heads and a shower of grey and white feathers rained down on them as the birds rose high above the rafters.

Delphine thought they were alone, but she was wrong. The headlights of a car blinded her as they came on without warning.

There was the click of a door latch. The back passenger door opened, swinging out slowly. She saw a shiny black shoe and expensive trousers, then the whole man emerged, unfolding himself carefully.

'Ah, Mademoiselle Harvey! We meet at last. The first time was hardly a social occasion.'

Delphine squinted into the white glare and peered through dancing dust motes to see the owner of the gravelly, American voice. She saw a red glow and there was a smell of sweet cigar smoke.

As he drew deeply on the cigar she caught the flash of a white shirt cuff and the brighter flash of gold.

'I think you must be mistaken,' Delphine said, amazed that her voice sounded so steady while her heart was cartwheeling inside her chest. 'I don't recall that we've ever met.'

'Don't lie to me, young woman.' The voice was low and sibilant. 'Armitage told me all about it, how you witnessed me carrying out a certain piece of business. You really ought to be more careful whom you trust, my dear.'

Delphine's heart gave a little flip. So, Mr Armitage really was involved on the seamier side of the law, as Mark had told her.

He had seemed such a nice old man. But then, Gaston had also seemed nice, in his way, and he had turned out bad, too.

Paul Dulac was the one she had been unable to trust and he had almost got himself killed saving her life. And poor Mark who, like her, was an innocent victim, was almost certainly dead. This whole affair was turning out to be a complete nightmare.

'You'll never get away with it,' she said and heard the stranger laugh softly and menacingly. 'Commissaire Dulac will know what's happened. He'll be after you for murder and kidnapping and . . . '

The American's laughter was becoming loud and hearty as if he had suddenly remembered a good joke recently heard.

'The commissaire will certainly know what has happened. In fact . . . '

He broke off and they all stood in the silence of the barn with the doves making their broody noises overhead and the storm raging outside.

Then she heard it, the crunch of feet falling heavily on wet gravel. In the distance a dog howled.

Delphine turned and hope flooded into her as she saw Paul Dulac framed in the wide barn doorway.

'Paul!' She gasped his name and started towards him, but was prevented from going any farther by Gaston. 'Paul, this is the man I saw kill the businessman in the alley . . . '

'Be quiet, stupid girl!' the American

shouted at her and then he was brushing past her, the cloying smell of his expensive cologne moving with him like an aura.

'Dulac! Good to see you. I hope that shoulder of yours isn't giving you too much pain. I figure Gaston here needs to do some target practice. Are you fit enough to travel? We have a long journey ahead of us.'

14

The two men shook hands warmly as if they were old friends. Delphine's mouth dropped open as she watched. It wasn't possible, she told herself. This was just too much beyond belief.

'I'm fine, Monsieur Borgheza,' Paul was saying, then he cast a jaundiced eye over Gaston Lacoste. 'No thanks to this fool here.'

'Yeah,' the American said, giving the other Frenchman a languid look. 'When I ordered him to kill the girl I thought he was a pretty good marksman. He botched that job up good, didn't he? Maybe we should finish him off here and now. What do you say, Dulac? Should I put a bullet in him, like that idiot nephew of Armitage's?'

Paul looked across at Gaston coldly, his eyes flitting only briefly over Delphine's stricken face.

'I don't know, Mr Borgheza. He could be useful to us.'

'Nonsense! He's already made one mistake too many. The girl we need, but this moron would serve us better dead.'

Delphine felt Gaston quake and his hands fell away from her as the American took out a tiny but lethal-looking pistol and started to raise it.

'Allow me, Monsieur Borgheza,' Paul said and Delphine saw the flash and heard the crack before she even saw the gun in his hand.

Beside her, she heard Gaston gasp then he fell against her, nearly knocking her over, before sinking to his knees and finally falling on to his face in a mess of mud, straw and rank-smelling dove guano.

Delphine felt her mouth go cold and dry and she thought she was going to faint. She could see Paul Dulac staring at her, his eyes piercing her like black daggers.

Anger rose in her like a tidal wave, bringing with it enough adrenalin to keep her on her feet and conscious.

'You're really despicable after all,' she said to him through gritted teeth. 'And I thought you were special.'

He tossed her a careless smile.

'I am sorry to disappoint you. Now, get in the car. We have business to see to before we say our final goodbyes.'

Delphine stood her ground and held her head up high, though her knees were beginning to buckle and the rest of her body seemed to have lost all contact with reality, together with her brain.

'I can't imagine what business there is that requires my help,' she stuttered. 'If you're going to kill me, you might as well do it now because you'll get nothing out of me.'

For a big man with a bullet hole in him, Paul Dulac moved incredibly quickly. Before she knew where she was, Delphine had his fingers digging into her arm and she was being bundled into the back seat of her car. The door slammed shut when he got in beside her.

The man called Borgheza climbed into the front passenger seat beside a uniformed driver who had not made a sound or a movement the whole time they had been there.

'All right, Dulac?'

'All right, Monsieur Borgheza. She won't cause any trouble. I give you my word.'

Delphine opened her mouth to object, but shut it again with a snap when she saw Paul's pistol pointing directly at her midriff and saw the determined look in his expression.

★　★　★

When they arrived at the hotel where Delphine had been a guest for such a short time, Tony Borgheza marched in ahead of them as if he owned the place and preceded them into the elevator, then along the corridor to Delphine's room, which had been booked for a fortnight, so it was still waiting for her return.

All the way, Paul held her tightly to his side, so that she could feel the muscles of his torso and thigh moving against her.

Once inside the room, the American locked the door behind them and pocketed the key.

Delphine turned from one to the other of them, shaking her head. She hadn't the faintest idea what they wanted from her.

'Look, this is ridiculous,' she told them with spread hands and shrugging shoulders. 'Why have you brought me here?'

Paul was searching the room methodically while Tony Borgheza, in his cream linen suit and heavy gold jewellery, looked on lazily like a venomous serpent that might strike at any moment.

'What did he give you, Delphine?' Paul asked.

'Who?'

'Armitage. He must have given you something. You were the only person, other than his nephew, whom he spoke to while he was here.'

'He didn't give me anything. Why would he? I was a perfect stranger to him. Anyway, wouldn't he put it in the hotel safe, whatever it was, if it was something valuable?'

Tony Borgheza shook his head.

'No, he would never do that. None of my people trusts hotel safes. Besides, it's not so easy to remove things in a hurry. Damn it, Dulac, the girl's got to be lying. It's here somewhere. We searched the nephew's room, found nothing!'

'Think, Delphine! There's got to be something!'

Paul was beginning to look impatient.

'I told you, he didn't give me . . . '

Delphine's hand flew to her mouth.

'Oh!'

'What?'

'There was something. I . . . '

Delphine looked about her, wishing the fog would clear from her brain.

'The first evening — he was a little

unwell, so he went up to his room halfway through dinner. He left something behind and I meant to return it to him, but I forgot all about it.'

'What, for goodness' sake?' It was Tony Borgheza who rushed forward and shook her roughly by the shoulders.

'Let her speak, Monsieur Borgheza,' Paul intervened. 'After we have the list I will deal with her.'

'What list?' Delphine asked, completely at a loss. 'It wasn't a list he left behind. It was just a guidebook. He had been showing me some places he thought I might be interested in visiting. It wasn't important, so I didn't worry about giving it back to him.'

Delphine looked about her, thinking hard, trying to remember what she had done with the colourful little booklet that Mr Armitage had shown her. If she gave it to them maybe they would go away and leave her alone.

Then she remembered. The bedside cabinet had been standing on uneven floor tiles and rattled at every move, so she had tucked the booklet underneath one of the legs. It had been exactly the right thickness.

'There!' she said, pointing to it.

Tony Borgheza swooped on it, pulled out a loose leaf of paper and held it up triumphantly.

'Well, then, Dulac. Now that I have Armitage's list of my operators in Europe, I trust I can leave you to — shall we say — clean up.'

He was looking at Delphine and there was no doubt in her mind what he was expecting Paul to do.

And, unlike Gaston before him, he wasn't going to miss, not at point blank range.

15

'I don't know whether it's all terribly romantic or completely mad! After everything that happened to you, I can't imagine why you should want to ever go back to France!'

Delphine shook her head and laughed at her mother, who was a nervous traveller at the best of times, but perhaps today she had reason to be nervous.

Her sister Meg, and friend, Joanne, giggled together across the aisle as the plane prepared to land at Nice. They were almost as excited as she was at the prospect of a wedding in the South of France.

'I just hope you know what you're doing,' her father said with a small frown and she leaned over and gave his hand a reassuring pat.

'Believe me, Dad, I couldn't be more sure.'

'We just want you to be happy,' her mother said, her eyes moist and her bottom lip quivering slightly.

'I know, Mum.'

⋆ ⋆ ⋆

The plane touched down and cruised along the length of the Tarmac before coming to rest outside the airport terminal building.

Delphine's stomach churned just a little, but it wasn't a fearful churning. This time, everything was going to be just perfect.

She couldn't believe that a whole year had gone by since that fateful holiday that had been planned to get her away from it all. Almost a year to the day, actually.

Not that this was her first return visit. She had been required to stay over for a while so that all the police business could be cleared up. And she had gone back to see Mark. She had gone back several times.

Dear Mark. The American's bullet had not killed him after all, but had seriously wounded him.

For weeks he had hung on between life and death, then his recuperation had been painfully slow, but he had made it in the end.

Of course, he had had to clear himself with the police, being the nephew of a hired assassin. But justice had not only been done, it had been seen to be done.

He walked away with a clean bill of health and a very clean legal slate. He had testified alongside Delphine and they had been rewarded by seeing not only Tony Borgheza but the whole of his widespread gangster network put behind bars.

* * *

'You can't wait to see him, can you?'

Meg was hanging on to her arm, her eyes excitedly scanning the crowds that milled about the airport arrivals area.

'That's about right,' Delphine confirmed, her cheeks dimpling and growing warm with anticipation.

'I've never seen you so much in love. He must be pretty special.'

'Oh, he is. I think I knew right from the start, but then, as you know, the world turned upside down on me and I couldn't see the mist for the fog.'

'You're so lucky, Sis!'

'You don't have to tell me, Meg.'

Delphine suddenly stuck her hand in the air and waved madly.

'Oh, look! There's Mark!'

He saw her at the same time and waved back. She ran to greet him and he hugged her tightly.

'Hi, Delphine. I was beginning to think you'd got cold feet.'

She threw her head back and laughed.

'Nonsense! The plane was late in taking off due to bad weather conditions over the Channel.'

Mark was greeting her parents, her sister and her best friend and they were all hugging and laughing together.

'Well, thank goodness the bad weather hasn't followed us over,' Delphine's father was saying, eyeing the bright sunshine and the blue sky as they walked in a tight group through the carpark.

'No, I'd say it's a perfect day for a wedding,' Mark said jovially, giving Delphine another hug and a kiss on the cheek.

'He really is so nice,' Joanne whispered in Delphine's ear.

'I'm glad you think so.'

Delphine gave a sideline glance in Mark's direction. He was looking tired and she hoped he hadn't been overdoing things.

During the last few weeks he had taken it upon himself to make all the wedding arrangements and he had promised her a very special day.

'Right,' he told them as they all packed themselves into his big silver Alpha Romeo and he manoeuvred his way through the late-morning traffic that was just as terrifying as London or

Paris in the rush hour.

'I've booked us all into a small hotel, just for an hour. There'll be time to shower and change, then the wedding will take place — um — well, somewhere quieter.'

'Oh, Mark, what a gem you are!' Delphine wanted to hug him, but she didn't want to distract him from his excellent driving and, besides, her sister was wedged between them, making physical contact impossible.

'I hope you'll think I'm still a gem this time tomorrow,' he said, shooting her a smile and everyone laughed. 'After all, surprises can so easily go wrong.'

'According to my daughter, Mark,' Delphine's father leaned forward and patted Mark's shoulder, 'you can do no wrong in her eyes. Lucky fella, eh?'

'Well, that's debatable. If I'd had my way . . .'

He broke off and concentrated on the driving. Delphine stared at her hands, clasped nervously in her lap.

She knew what he was thinking, but at the end of the day, there hadn't been any real choice. She had followed the dictates of her heart.

★ ★ ★

No sooner had they refreshed themselves and changed into their official wedding outfits, than they were on the road again, but this time, Mark had hired two white Daimler wedding cars to take them to where it was all going to happen.

Delphine was bursting with love, happiness and excitement. She thought that she would never be able to control herself before they were pronounced husband and wife.

Nothing, absolutely nothing, was going to spoil this day, she thought as she inspected herself for the last time in the full-length mirror in her room.

Her hands smoothed down the long, straight skirt of her creamy satin dress. A final adjustment to the orange blossom hair ornament and she was ready. She picked up her bouquet of pink and mauve bougainvillea flowers and took a deep breath.

★ ★ ★

The scenery started to change from the blue and gold coastline and its busy tourist trade to red earth and green undulating hills and plains. Outside, the day was scorchingly hot, but the air-conditioning in the cars was blissfully cool. Even so, Delphine felt her palms grow sweaty with anticipation.

'Oh, dear!' Her stomach had just taken off as though they were on a roller coaster at a fairground.

Joanne, who was sitting with her, gave her hand a squeeze.

'Don't worry. It'll soon be over and you'll be a married lady.'

'Funny! That wasn't what I was thinking about.'

'You were thinking about him,' Joanne whispered. 'I can always tell.

Steam comes out of your ears.'

'Really, Joanne!'

'It's true, I'm telling you.'

On the other side of her, Meg turned around and grinned.

'I still can't see you being a farmer's wife.'

'I can't see her future husband being a farmer, but . . . ' Joanne shrugged and they all giggled like schoolgirls out on a spree.

'You know,' Meg said, 'when they talk about life being nothing like all those romantic novels you read — well, I used to think it was true, but you've just proved them wrong, Delphine.'

'Yes,' Delphine breathed with an ecstatic smile. 'Haven't I just!'

'This is really happening, isn't it?' Joanne wanted to know, screwing up her face and actually pinching her own arm. 'I mean, we're not all having the same wonderful dream, are we?'

They all exchanged glances and the laughter took off once more.

Delphine settled herself back in the

plush leather seat with a sigh and tried to will herself to relax.

'He is going to be there, isn't he?'

Mark looked at her over his shoulder from the front seat.

'Well, he wasn't exactly sent an official invitation, but I think he'll probably turn up anyway.'

'Oh, don't!'

There was panic in her voice as she felt the icy finger of fate tracing a menacing pattern over her warm flesh and goose pimples rose by the million making her shiver convulsively while her cheeks burned.

'Let's talk of something else, shall we?'

★ ★ ★

The scenery was becoming oddly familiar as the cars ploughed their way through miles of lavender fields and olive groves and suddenly Delphine knew what Mark had done. She caught his knowing smile through the rear mirror and saw him give a small nod.

'Here we are, then,' he said a few minutes later as they whispered to a stop by a diamond-studded stream.

She recognised the place where Paul had taken her for a picnic.

In the distance she could just make out the top of the red pantile roof of the Lacoste farm. But it was the little group of people who were already gathered in the clearing surrounded by olive trees that took Delphine's interest most of all.

Most of them she knew well by now. Some of them she looked forward to getting to know in the very near future.

'Come on, Delphine,' Mark said, gently taking her hand and leading her forward. 'Everything's ready and every-one's here.'

'Everyone?' Her voice quavered slightly, her eyes anxiously scanning the crowd.

16

The group parted to let them through and then she saw him, by the side of the plump, jovial priest. He sported a white gardenia in his lapel and his expression was every bit as anxious as hers.

He stepped forward with the same urgency that Delphine was having difficulty controlling in her own heart. Here was the man she was about to marry, Paul Dulac.

Paul gripped her hands and kissed her on each cheek and there was a ripple of whispered conversation among the spectators.

'You are on time,' he said.

'The English are always on time,' she told him with a wicked grin and they turned to the priest so that their union could be made official.

★ ★ ★

The Latin words that were pronounced floated into the air above Delphine's head. Her mind was looking back, seeing everything that had led up to this day in minute flashes of hazy memory.

Paul's last assignment had been an undercover one and the most important of his career. He had taken Gaston with him, because he was the only man he knew he could trust.

It was a lucky thing that Paul had thought to load one pistol with blanks the night of the storm.

Gaston deserved an Oscar for his portrayal of a dead man, especially since he could so easily have taken a real bullet from Tony Borgheza's gun.

In the end it had been a gun with real bullets pointed at the American. He didn't take it seriously until several more French undercover police appeared out of the shadows, all armed to the teeth and backing up Paul in the final coup of his career.

Even so, it had taken some time to convince Delphine which side Paul was really on and that she was safe from any further danger. Thanking him for saving her life had been difficult. She felt foolish, having doubted him. Paul had simply smiled his melting smile and reminded her that he was only doing his job.

She forgave him, but her heart was heavy as she watched him walk away, as she thought, for the last time. But he had come back. And kept on coming back until he wore her down and there was nothing she wanted more than to be Mrs Paul Dulac.

★　★　★

The priest finally fell silent and waited patiently, his head to one side, a benign expression on his soft pink face. Delphine glanced down at the third finger on her left hand and saw a narrow gold band encrusted with diamonds. She hadn't even been aware of it going on, but there it was.

'Are we married?' she asked Paul in a

stunned whisper and he nodded.

'You are not regretting it already, I hope.'

'Oh, no,' she told him. 'This is the one day in my life I shall never, ever regret.'

'I promise you many more, my love, but for now, kiss me.'

She kissed him to the loud cheers of all their guests, then they moved at the head of a long procession through the lavender fields with their heads filled with perfume and their hearts full of happiness.

★ ★ ★

Just over the rise there was another red roof. In fact, there were a series of undulating roofs above white painted stone walls and now the air was tinged with the smell of oranges and lemons and limes.

In a wide courtyard, a white open-ended marquee was set up with long trestle tables filled with an array of food and wine. A trio of musicians was playing — guitar, accordion and piano.

150

The romantic traditional music of Provence floated over to them on the warm breeze.

It was Mark who led the way, claiming he was anxious to get his best man speech over so they could all relax and drink themselves silly.

Delphine knew how hard it was for him, knowing that he could never be her groom. He had asked her to marry him while he was still prone in his hospital bed, though he always claimed he knew he never stood a chance.

Paul wrapped his arms around her as they watched their combined families join happily together. Dogs and children played joyfully in the sun, while cats stretched lazily on window ledges and flowers tumbled gaily out of barrels and boxes. It was as though she was being given a glimpse into her future and she liked what she saw.

'Welcome home, Delphine,' Paul whispered in her ear and she melted into him, her heart spilling over with love.

We do hope that you have enjoyed reading this large print book.

Did you know that all of our titles are available for purchase?

We publish a wide range of high quality large print books including:
Romances, Mysteries, Classics
General Fiction
Non Fiction and Westerns

Special interest titles available in large print are:
The Little Oxford Dictionary
Music Book, Song Book
Hymn Book, Service Book

Also available from us courtesy of Oxford University Press:
Young Readers' Dictionary
(large print edition)
Young Readers' Thesaurus
(large print edition)

For further information or a free brochure, please contact us at:
Ulverscroft Large Print Books Ltd.,
The Green, Bradgate Road, Anstey,
Leicester, LE7 7FU, England.
Tel: (00 44) 0116 236 4325
Fax: (00 44) 0116 234 0205

SO GOLDEN THEIR HARVEST

Jane Carrick

Susan and Hazel had looked after their father since their mother's death, but now Susan is to marry Colin, a farmer, and move to Australia. However, after Colin's Gran has a fall, the old lady begs him to take over her run-down farm in Scotland instead. Susan doesn't mind and works hard with Colin to build up the farm. Peter, one of the farm hands, falls in love with Susan, but she has eyes only for Colin. When Hazel visits Susan, she finds herself attracted to the handsome Peter, but he tells her of his love for her sister.